ALPHA 2 DELTA

SSG. JOHN MARKEWICZ

Alpha 2 Delta by John Markewicz

Alpha 2 Delta by John Markewicz

DEDICATED TO ALL THE SOLDIERS AND ALL THE WAR STORIES I EVER HEARD AROUND EVERY CAMP FIRE OR ON EVERY NIGHT OF STAFF DUTY NCO OR CHARGE OF QUARTERS OR CQ RUNNER OR ON ANY OF A THOUSAND NIGHTS IN THE NCO CLUB OR FLIGHT OPERATIONS.

Alpha 2 Delta by John Markewicz

INTRODUCTION:

YA' KNOW THE DIFFERENCE BETWEEN A WAR STORY AND A FAIRY TALE?

A FAIRYTALE STARTS OUT: "ONCE UPON A TIME."

A WAR STORY STARTS OUT: "THIS IS NO SHIT!"

OTHER THAN THAT, THEY ARE EXACTLY THE SAME!!!

THIS ONE SHOULD START WITH "ONCE UPON A TIME," ENJOY.

Alpha 2 Delta by John Markewicz

Alpha 2 Delta by John Markewicz

CHAPTER 1

WHAT'S AN A TEAM?

Brigadier General Marcus Boyd is agitated, he is pacing in his luxurious office. Being the Senior Public Information Officer for U.S. Army Special Forces is a pain in the ass. Nearly everything they do is classified! Can't tell anybody a dam thing about anything. Now the Boy Scouts of America want a demonstration of Green Beret capabilities.

Where the hell is he going to find a spare A Team?

A Special Forces Operational Detachment Alpha or A Team, is the primary fighting force of the Green Berets.

Green Beret A Teams are made up of 12 men, each with a separate Military Occupational Specialty (MOS). Each A - Team member is cross-trained in other specialties.

A typical 12-man A Team comprises:

1 Detachment Commander
The Commander is the team leader and is responsible for outfitting his team, organizing missions and briefing the unit on mission objectives.

1 Assistant Detachment Commander
The Assistant Detachment Commander assists the team's Commander, ready to take over command if needed. If the team splits into two teams, the Assistant Detachment Commander commands the second team.

1 Operations Sergeant, the Special Forces Operations Sergeant is responsible for the overall organization, functionality and training of a Special Forces team. He makes sure the team is outfitted correctly and supports the team commander.

Alpha 2 Delta by John Markewicz

1 Assistant Operations Sergeant plus Intelligence Sergeant this team member ensures that the team has all the equipment and supplies needed to perform the mission. He also gathers and analyzes mission-critical intelligence.

2 Weapons Sergeants, Special Forces Weapons Sergeants are experts in a wide range of American and foreign made weapons systems. They are proficient in the operation and tactical employment of a wide range of weapons systems, including all US light weapons, from pistols and rifles up to .50 caliber M2 Browning machine gun, heavy weapons such as the 60mm, 80mm, and 120mm mortars, anti-tank missile systems such as the Javelin, light artillery, and anti-aircraft missiles such as the Stinger. They are also well-versed with equivalent foreign weapon systems.

2 Communications Sergeants, Special Forces Communications Sergeants are proficient in a wide range of radio communications equipment and antennas used in the field, they understand everything from morse code to encrypted satellite transmissions plus they have an in depth understanding of computer Information Technology; Internet/Web, telecommunications, computing & computer science, hardware, software, etc.

2 Medical Sergeants, Special Forces Medical Sergeants are considered to be the finest first-response/trauma medical technicians in the world. Though they're primarily trained with an emphasis on trauma medicine, they also have a working knowledge of dentistry, veterinary care, public sanitation, water quality and optometry. The ability of Special Forces Medical Sergeants to treat the medical problems of a local populations is a valuable component of counter insurgency operations.

2 Engineering Sergeants, Special Forces Engineering Sergeants are the guys you go to when you want something built or destroyed.

Alpha 2 Delta by John Markewicz

They are experts in explosive demolition. As a demolition specialist, the engineer sergeant can carry out demolition raids against enemy targets, such as bridges, railroads, fuel depots, buildings, dams, and other structures, and/or critical components of infrastructure. Special Forces Engineers are also experts in military or civil construction and can carry out a range of projects from building military fortifications to civil engineering tasks such as create bridges, construct buildings, digging wells or fabricating a medical clinic using only materials available at hand.

Oddly enough, at this very moment, in an old-World War II open bay barracks is a collection of older Special Forces soldiers. They are doing hash and trash duties and details (various minor work assignments) for the Post Sergeant Major and Post Commander at Fort Bragg, North Carolina while they are finishing out their last hitch prior to retirement and being processed out of the active-duty Army.

In an old second world war style barracks there are no urinals. Just a long ceramic trough that has a water pipe running along the top edge. The pipe has holes drilled in it and water runs into the trough thru these holes continuously. It's first thing in the morning. Sergeants Lucas and Green the team weapons specialists are standing at the trough taking a leak. Just as they are finishing and turning toward the six sinks mounted on the opposite wall, Sergeant Green says aloud for all to hear "Dam that water cold this mornin'." All the other Sergeants in the latrine are saying "YEA, YOU WISH!!"

Enter in the main barracks area, Second Lieutenant Melissa Boyd. Discharge Processing Officer, Fort Bragg, North Carolina Military Personnel Office and General Marcus Boyd's' niece.

All the retiring Special Forces soldiers in this group are going to receive the Army Distinguished Service Medal. The fourth highest award a soldier can receive. The award certificates are to be signed by a General Grade Officer. Second Lieutenant Melissa Boyd decides to see Brigadier General Marcus Boyd for those signatures.

Sitting in her Uncles office Second Lieutenant Melissa Boyd explains to General Boyd why these soldiers have been recommended to receive these awards. Each soldier has at least 30 years of service, each has multiple awards for exceptional bravery and dedication to duty plus fidelity and loyalty to the United States of America and the United States Army in addition to their incredibly meritorious service spanning four decades. They have all received one final promotion prior to retiring as directed by the Special Forces Commander. SFC Green and SFC Jakes have received two promotions to get them back into a reasonable retirement pay grade following Field Grade Article 15's (The authority for commanders to give an Article 15 is found in what is called Article 15 of the Uniform Code of Military Justice. An Article 15 is considered non-judicial punishment, meaning that it is not considered a judicial proceeding. Non-judicial punishment is a military justice option available to commanders. It permits commanders to resolve allegations of minor misconduct against a soldier without resorting to higher forms of discipline, such as a court-martial the decision to impose an Article 15 is completely the commanders. A soldier may, however, refuse to accept the Article 15 and instead demand trial by court-martial.) that resulted in a demotion to Sergeant E-5 and forfeiture of two months pay for public drunkenness and brawling in which some civilians were injured.

{Think Master Sergeant Jakes and Master Sergeant Green throwing a civilian thru the door to the bar and him landing out in the street then stealing a whole roast beef and handing back and forth to gnaw on while driving back to post and being arrested by the Military Police.}

Alpha 2 Delta by John Markewicz

They have all served in the Gulf War, The Somali Civil War, The Intervention in Haiti, The Kosovo War, and Operation Infinite Reach in Afghanistan.

Though every one of them is at least 50 years old each is in exceptional physical condition due to their extensive physical training regimen.

Brigadier General Boyd reviews the requirements to qualify as a Green Beret mentally:

1. You must be a U.S. citizen

2. You must be at least 20 years old by your ship date to Infantry One Station Unit Training (OSUT) and not have reached your 32nd birthday prior to the same ship date

3. You must be an active duty or Army National Guard Soldier

4. You must qualify for airborne training

5. You must meet the Physical Fitness Assessment (PFA) minimum standard of 49 pushups, 59 sit-ups, 15:12 (two-mile run), six pull-ups

6. You must be eligible for a Secret security clearance

Brigadier General Marcus Boyd begins to smile more and more as he reads the names.

Special Forces Weapons Specialist: Master Sergeant Bill Lucas

Special Forces Weapons Specialist: Sergeant First Class Nathan Green

Special Forces Communications Specialist: Master Sergeant Tyler Black

Special Forces Communications Specialist: Master Sergeant Nick Gronski

Alpha 2 Delta by John Markewicz

Special Forces Medical Specialist: Master Sergeant Johnny Allen

Special Forces Engineering Specialist: Master Sergeant Jack Taylor

Special Forces Engineering Specialist: Sergeant First Class Martin Jakes

Special Forces Detachment Commander Lieutenant Colonel Arthur Darlington

Special Forces Assistant Detachment Commander Chief Warrant Officer 5 Dean Smith

Special Forces Operations Sergeant: Sergeant Major Tom Roberts

Special Forces Intel Sergeant: First Sergeant Mike Watters

Second Lieutenant Melissa Boyd is walking into the World War II barracks with a stack of orders. She begins calling out names and handing each man a copy of the orders.

Lt. Col. Darlington: "What the hell is this?"

Second Lieutenant Melissa Boyd: "New TDY (Temporary Duty) Orders Sir and by the way General Boyd has instructed that Staff Sergeant Amitola a newly minted Special Forces Medic is assigned to you to fill out the team roster."

{Staff Sergeant Amitola is full blooded Kiowa Indian. Her name means Rainbow and her beauty is remarkable.}

Lt. Col. Darlington: "We're all going to a Boy Scout Jamboree in Idaho – For A Freakin' Week?"

Sergeant First Class Green: "No, Oh Hell NO! I been thru every rotten assignment in every third world shit hole on this planet AND NOW THAT I'M RETIREIN' NOW THEY STICKIN ME WITH THE BOY SCOUTS"

COMPLETE SILENCE!

Alpha 2 Delta by John Markewicz

Then in unison the rest of the team says: "WELL WE'RE GLAD TO SEE YOU'RE NOT BITTER ABOUT IT!!!"

The entire team including Sergeant Green laughs uncontrollably!

Operations Sergeant/1st Sergeant Watters hands some paperwork to Sergeant Major Roberts.

Sergeant Major Roberts: "OK, LISTEN UP!! Everybody load up now, this will be a HALO (High Altitude Low Opening) parachute drop into Farragut State Park, Idaho. Followed by one week in the field to demonstrate the abilities of the Green Beret to the Boy Scouts of America, no live ammo, lots of blanks and pyrotechnics and Blue Band Weapons/Explosives. Our Call Sign: Alfa 2 Delta. Aviation support will be monitoring our frequency and will be available on day seven late in the afternoon only for extraction or medical emergency Callsign Ghostrider.

Should it become necessary Sergeants Lucas, Taylor, Gronski, Allen and Sergeant Major Roberts, plus Chief Smith as commander are on Ghost team. Sergeants Amitola, Green, Black, Jakes, Watters, and Lt. Col. Darlington as commander are on Shadow team.

Everybody standing tall, wall to wall and on your best behavior!

 I WANT TO UN-FUCK THIS THING BEFORE IT EVER GETS STARTED!

QUESTIONS?"

The barracks is completely silent.

Sergeant Major Roberts: "Good let's roll! Asses on the tarmac in 60"

CHAPTER 2

HOW'D WE GET HERE?

A Boeing C-17 Globemaster III aircraft is spooling up its engines sitting on the tarmac at Pope Air Force Base, North Carolina.

The C-17 Globemaster III is the most flexible cargo aircraft to enter the airlift force. The C-17 is capable of rapid strategic delivery of troops and all types of cargo to main operating bases or directly to forward bases in the deployment area. The aircraft can perform tactical airlift and airdrop missions and can transport litters and ambulatory patients during aeromedical evacuations. The inherent flexibility and performance of the C-17 force improve the ability of the total airlift system to fulfill the worldwide air mobility requirements of the United States.

The ultimate measure of airlift effectiveness is the ability to rapidly project and sustain an effective combat force close to a potential battle area. Threats to U.S. interests have changed in recent years, and the size and weight of U.S.-mechanized firepower and equipment have grown in response to improved capabilities of potential adversaries. This trend has significantly increased air mobility requirements, particularly in the area of large or heavy outsize cargo. As a result, newer and more flexible airlift aircraft are needed to meet potential armed contingencies, peacekeeping or humanitarian missions worldwide. The C-17 is capable of meeting today's demanding airlift missions.

The team walks up the ramp onto the aircraft and they pick a spot and relax into the troop seats along the inside fuselage walls of the aircraft.

The ramp closes as the aircraft begins to taxi to the active runway.

Some of the guys open a paperback book, some open a favorite letter they always carry, some are looking at a map, some guys are thumbing through an X rated magazine, and some are reading the newspaper.

Five hours later the lights inside the aircraft change from white to red.

Alpha 2 Delta by John Markewicz

Everyone puts their oxygen masks on.

Time to go. The blast of cold air as the ramp goes down on the C-17 Globemaster III is frigid.

The morning light is just starting to streak pink and light blue slightly ahead of the dark purple horizon.

Sergeant Major Roberts lifts his mask, screaming: "Stand Up, Check the Equipment of The Man in Front of You, Move Out!"

 The team heads for the ramp and jumps out one at a time as the Jumpmaster taps each man on the shoulder to indicate his approval to jump.

(*Military Free Fall parachuting allows Special Operations Forces personnel to deploy their parachutes at a predetermined altitude, assemble in the air, navigate under canopy, and land safely together as a tactical unit ready to execute their mission. Although free-fall parachuting can produce highly accurate landings, it is primarily a means of entering a designated impact area within the objective area. The following are two basic types of Military Free Fall operations:*
• High-altitude low-opening (HALO) operations are jumps made with an exit altitude of up to 35,000 feet mean sea level (MSL) and a parachute deployment altitude at or below 6,000 feet above ground level (AGL). HALO infiltrations are the preferred Military Free Fall method of infiltration when the enemy air defense posture is not a viable threat to the infiltration platform. HALO infiltrations require the infiltration platform to fly within several kilometers of the drop zone.)

The explosion of thunder is deafening and the team is instantly in the clouds, the rain stings any exposed skin and the turbulence throws their bodies into frightening positions. The team members try to turn on their backs so the equipment takes the brunt of the stinging rain. They are spun and swirled and bounced and even beatin' nearly to death by some hail. Exiting the clouds, the team members parachute's open and they glide silently into calm, sunny daylight with beautiful blue skies.

Alpha 2 Delta by John Markewicz

Landing on a beautiful, grassy open plain the team checks themselves and their equipment, they roll up their chutes and gather for a post action brief.

They look around to see a group of Indians on horseback approaching them.

Lt. Col Darlington turns and starts walking toward the Indians: "Looks like we ruined somebody's movie scene."

CW5 Smith, walking toward the Indians, waving his arms, yelling: "SORRY, WE'RE VERY SORRY!!"

An arrow zips past his head and a second arrow grazes his shoulder!

CW5 Smith:" DEFENSIVE POSITIONS!!"

Lt. Col. Darlington: "Now, what the hell? Are they crazy?"

The hissing zip of a rifle bullet passing his head convinces him to hit the deck.

Lt. Col Darlington and CW5 Smith have their Beretta 92F, 9MM pistols but no ammo and cannot defend themselves.

Instantly Weapons, Communication, Engineers and Medics sections are sitting cross legged, kneeling or lying prone, some men are using their packs as support for their rifles.

Sergeant Major Roberts: "DELTA HIT THE DECK!"

Lt. Col. Darlington and CW5 Smith try to get lower to the ground but their uniform buttons are in the way.

U.S. Army M-4A1's open fire and half a dozen Indians drop instantly.

Lt. Col Darlington and CW5 Smith roll over and throw flash - bangs.

Alpha 2 Delta by John Markewicz

The shocking explosion of the Flash – Bangs results in horses rearing, riders being thrown, horses running wildly and scattering in all directions.

The attack is broken up and the Indians that are still able to do so retreat, running hell bent for leather away from the Green Berets!

Lt. Col. Darlington on intercom: "CHECK FIRE!"

Sergeant Major Roberts on intercom: "NO ONE IS SUPPOSED TO HAVE LIVE AMMO!"

First Sergeant Watters, under his breath: "Good thing nobody listens."

Lt. Col. Darlington yelling at the running Indians: "What the hell was that all about?"

Suddenly, the team hears noises on the other side of a grove of trees and they take up defensive positions once again. Nerves on edge, every eye and ear strains to identify a new threat. Fingers lightly rest on triggers; icy calm comes over the team as each man prepares to defend himself.

Lt. Col. Darlington gives nearly silent orders via internal intercom and hand signals for Weapons Sergeants Green and Lucas to recon the area of the trees to identify the threat.

Sergeants Lucas and Green move out silently.

They return to the team in short order and explain it is an 1800's wagon train on the other side of the grove of trees next to a river.

Col. Darlington: "A wagon train!?"

Master Sergeant Green: 'Yes Sir, horses, oxen, wooden wagons, wooden wheels, canvas covers, no antennas, no lights, no electronics visible of any kind, no distinctive markings, no heavy weapons.

Alpha 2 Delta by John Markewicz

Master Sergeant Lucas: "Some of the people are injured. Looks like battle damage to the wagons and various physical injuries to multiple individuals and some of the animals."

The team quickly discusses the situation, they decide they cannot allow the injured to go untreated or perhaps die while they have the power to save them.

The team moves out silently, wide interval between men, toward the wagon train.

When they reach the edge of the grove of trees nearest the wagon train, they step out and warn the people to remain silent and not to move, the soldier's weapons are at the ready but not pointed at the civilians.

The civilians are startled and amazed but stay silent and still.

The people of the wagon train stare, gazes fixed on these strange people.

Team members notice a group of people murmuring, gathering around a person lying on the ground. Some of the people are crying, some are just shaking their heads

Communications Sergeant Gronski waving his hand: "MEDICS!"

The Special Forces Medical Team Sergeants Allen and Amitola jump into action. They are presented with a female that has a sucking chest wound.

Lt. Col. Darlington: "Who's in charge here?"

A man wearing a Confederate Cavalry hat steps forward: "Colonel Lightly, Cavalry of the Confederate States of America at your service, Sir."

Alpha 2 Delta by John Markewicz

Lt. Col Darlington: "Colonel Lightly I am Lt. Col. Darlington United States Army Special Forces. Tell your people to stand still, remain quiet, and keep their hands away from their weapons!"

Col. Lightly: "Ya'all heard the man! Now don't any of ya' dare do anything foolish!"

When the Medics arrive at Sergeant Gronski's side, they get the young ladies vitals then attended to the sucking chest wound, they remove the bullet, reinflate the lung, stitch up the wound, clean and bandage the site carefully then they start an IV with D5W and a strong pain reliever. They put an oxygen mask from one of the left-over HALO tanks on the patients face and set the flow of oxygen. This task completed they move through the crowd treating wounded civilians while Master Sergeant Gronski stays with the patient with the chest wound and does his best to comfort her.

Master Sergeant, Engineer Specialist Jack Taylor appears with a tree limb he has trimmed out to serve as Cynthia's IV tree.

A seriously wounded Cynthia Wayne/Lightly: "I am so frightened gentlemen, I believe that I am mortally wounded, Sir!"

Master Sergeant Gronski holding her hand: "Relax Ma'am you're going to be fine. Our Medics have never lost a man yet!"

Master Sergeant Taylor looking down at her as he hangs her IV bag on the tree limb he has made for the job: "Young Lady you have just been, inspected, injected, detected, selected, and accepted into the Special Forces medical care system and you getting' the best care anywhere. Don't you fret now!

Cynthia begins to relax and as the pain reliever takes effect, she soon closes her eyes and drifts off to sleep.

A young man with an arrow thru his forearm is the next patient to be treated by Staff Sergeant Amitola. They are both in their early twenties and they lock eyes momentarily as she begins to work.

Alpha 2 Delta by John Markewicz

She removes her helmet and the young man stammers, overcome by her beauty: "Mu - My name is MATT, that is; Matthew Nilsson, Ma'am."

I'm Staff Sergeant Amitola, Mr. Nilsson relax, this won't hurt; much. Staff Sergeant Amitola administers a local anesthetic and clips off the end of the arrow then removes the shaft. She cleans the wound and bandages the injury carefully.

Matthew is being extra brave and heroically controlling his emotions and working hard not to let tears well up in his eyes. He is doing his very best trying to impress her. Her smile and her gentle voice saying: "You'll be fine." sends young Matt's pride and hope and desire all sailing over the moon.

Master Sergeant Allen bending over to whisper in her ear: "He'd have to be dead three days to pry that smile off his face."

Staff Sergeant Amitola sarcastically: "Yea, Right!"

Master Sergeant Allen's next patient is a little girl approximately 10 years of age with a serious head laceration. Head lacerations bleed a lot and look scary but are usually not that serious. This one however is fairly bad and the patient is crying uncontrollably. Master Sergeant Allen using as gentle a voice as he can muster: "There, there now, you're going to be alright, I promise, plus if you're a good girl and stay still for just one moment I have a wonderful treat for you!" Master Sergeant Allen cleans the child up with some IV solution then uses a powder with a clotting agent in it to stop the flow of blood. Next, he cleans the wound area after which he uses medical super glue to close the wound and bandages it carefully. Finally, he gives his newest patient a hug and lollypop.

Master Sergeant Allen: "See that wasn't too bad now was it?"

Alpha 2 Delta by John Markewicz

He is paid for his services with an adorable, little girls smile, even though she is quite fixated on the cherry lollipop right at this moment.

Master Sergeant Allen and Staff Sergeant Amitola come together to work on their next patient a large horse with an arrow in its side. Staff Sergeant Amitola calms the animal while Master Sergeant Allen mixes an animal tranquilizer with some sugar from the packets in his MRE's. After the animal is dosed with medications Staff Sergeant Amitola helps to coax him to lie down and as soon as he is asleep the Special Forces Medics go to work. They clean the wound and surrounding area carefully. They expand the incision around the arrow head. They remove the arrow. Stitch up the wound and inject their patient with antibiotics

The rest of the injuries to people and animals are superficial cuts, bruises, and sprains. They are treated with a few stitches or butterfly closures and first aid cream plus band aids. Some patients are treated with a sports wrap bandage.

Some patients are issued non-aspirin pain relievers.

Alpha 2 Delta by John Markewicz

CHAPTER 3

SITUATION REPORT (SITREP)

Lt. Col. Darlington on internal intercom: "Chief what's our status?"

CW5 Smith: "Sir, all team members are present and available for duty. Six wounded civilians one seriously wounded equine. Each has been treated and all will survive. We are ready to move, however reference physical security, there will be traces of our visit here."

Lt. Col. Darlington turning to Colonel Lightly: "Col. Lightly as the ranking officer on site my team is at your disposal sir."

Col. Lightly: "In view of your obvious advanced knowledge, skills, and abilities and those of your soldiers I insist that you remain in command and determine your missions as you see fit sir."

Lt. Col. Darlington: "Thank you, Sir!"

CW5 Smith on intercom: "Col. Darlington – Mission Critical Briefing, Sir!"

Lt. Col. Darlington whispering into his intercom mic: "Roger that, Chief on my way what's your location? Turning to Colonel Lightly: Col. Lightly, if you'll excuse me Sir?"

Col. Lightly: "Of Course Sir."

CW5 Smith on intercom: The Team is gathered near the river approximately 500 meters north of the wagon train sir.

Lt. Col. Darlington arrives at the team's location.

CW5 Smith: "Commander – all communications are down, tablets/cell phones are inoperative, pluggers are inoperative, GPS systems on cell phones are inoperative. Sincgars, our primary communications radio is operational but we are unable to contact anyone. We have 8 full, live, 30 round magazines of 5.56 ball ammo for the M-4A1's, plus 24 full 30 round magazines of blank 5.56 ammo for the M-4A1's, 24 Grenade Simulators, 24 Artillery Simulators, 22 Flash Bangs, 24 Trip Flares, we have 36 Star Clusters: 12 Red, 12 Green, 12 White, 4 Thermite Grenades, and 48 Smoke grenades,12 red, 12 green, 12 black, 12 white, food can stretch seven days, potable water available, all weapons fully functional, medical supplies satisfactory, no Wounded In Action, no Killed In Action, no Missing In Action. Sir the Engineers have brought along assorted small civilian fireworks, Cherry Bombs, Sparklers, Firecrackers, Quarter Sticks, Roman Candles, etc."

{The AN/PS-11 Precision Lightweight Global Positioning System Receiver (PLGR Colloquially "Plugger") is a ruggedized, hand held, single frequency Global Positioning System Receiver fielded by the U.S. Military.}

[Single Channel Ground and Airborne Radio System (SINCGARS) is a Combat Net Radio (CNR) currently used by U.S. and allied military forces. The radios, which handle voice and data communications, are designed to be reliable, secure and easily maintained. Vehicle-mount, backpack, airborne, and handheld form factors are available. SINCGARS uses 25 kHz channels in the VHF FM band, from 30 to 87.975 MHz. It has single-frequency and frequency hopping modes. The frequency-hopping mode hops 111 times a second.]

Devices marked with a blue band are inert training items.

(*Smoke grenades are canister-type grenades used as ground-to-ground or ground-to-air signaling devices, target or landing zone marking devices, or as screening devices for unit movements. Smoke grenades are normally considered non-lethal, although incorrect use may cause death. The body consists of a sheet steel cylinder with a four emission holes on top and one on the bottom to allow smoke release when the grenade is ignited. The filler consists of 250 to 350 grams of colored (red, green, orange, gray, yellow, blue, white, black, or violet) smoke composition (mostly potassium chlorate, lactose, and a dye). The reaction is exothermic and grenade casings will often remain scalding hot for some time even after the grenade is no longer emitting smoke.*)

Military Star clusters are used for signaling and illuminating. They are issued in an expendable launcher, which consists of a launching tube and firing cap. These signals produce a cluster of five free-falling pyrotechnic stars. The current types of star clusters include the M125A1 (green star), the M158 (red star), and the M159 (white star).

Alpha 2 Delta by John Markewicz

Trip Flare is a device used by military forces to secure an area and to guard against infiltration. It consists of tripwire around the area, linked to one or more flares. When the tripwire is triggered, as by someone unsuspectingly disturbing it, the flare is activated and begins burning. The light from the flare simultaneously warns that the perimeter may have been breached and also gives light for investigating.

The M115A2 Artillery Ground Burst Simulator and M116A1 Hand Grenade Simulator simulate battle noises and battlefield effects – Whistling sound of shells in flight, ground burst explosions and/or grenades exploding.

A stun grenade, also known as a flash grenade, flashbang, thunder flash or sound bomb, is a less-lethal explosive device used to temporarily disorient an enemy's senses. It is designed to produce a blinding flash of light of around 7 megacandela (Mcd) and an intensely loud "bang" of greater than 170 decibels (dB). The flash momentarily activates all photoreceptor cells in the eye, blinding it for approximately five seconds. Afterward, victims perceive an afterimage which impairs their vision. The sheer volume of the detonation also causes temporary deafness in the victim and also disturbs the fluid in the ear, causing a loss of balance.

The AN-M14 TH3 incendiary hand grenade is used to destroy equipment. It can damage, immobilize, or destroy vehicles, weapons systems, shelters, or munitions. The grenade may also be used to start fires in areas containing flammable materials. The grenade can be thrown 25 meters by average soldier. A portion of the thermate mixture is converted to molten iron, which burns at 4,000 degrees Fahrenheit. It will fuze together the metallic parts of any object that it contacts. Thermate is an improved version of thermite, the incendiary agent used in hand grenades during World War II. The thermate filler of the AN-M14 grenade burns for 40 seconds and can burn through a 1/2-inch homogeneous steel plate. It produces its own oxygen and will burn under water.

ROMAN CANDLE: a traditional type of firework that ejects one or more stars or exploding shells. Roman candles come in a variety of sizes, from 6 mm (0.24 in) diameter for consumers, up to 8 cm (3.1 in) diameter in professional fireworks. Despite their name, Roman candles did not originate in Ancient Rome, or in Italy. Rather, they originated in China.

CHERRY BOMB: a round firecracker that makes a loud noise when it explodes.

Alpha 2 Delta by John Markewicz

QUARTER STICK: M-80 (explosive) from Wikipedia, the free encyclopedia

M-80s are an American class of large powerful firecrackers, sometimes called salutes.[1] M-80s were originally made in the mid 20th century for the U.S. military to simulate explosives or artillery fire; later, M-80s were manufactured as fireworks. Traditionally, M-80s were made from a small cardboard tube, often red, approximately 1 1/2 inches (3.8 cm) long and 9/16 inch (1.4 cm) inside diameter, with a fuse coming out of the side; this type of fuse is commonly known as cannon fuse or Visco fuse, after a company responsible for standardizing the product. The tubes usually hold approximately 3 grams of pyrotechnic flash powder.[2] The "M" is designated by a U.S. military convention for "standard" equipment and "80" is a non-meaningful ID number.

SPARKLER: a type of hand-held firework that burns slowly while emitting colored flames, sparks, and other visual effects.

FIRECRACKER: (cracker, noise maker, banger,) is a small explosive device primarily designed to produce a large amount of noise, especially in the form of a loud bang, usually for celebration or entertainment; any visual effect is incidental to this goal. They have fuses, and are wrapped in a heavy paper casing to contain the explosive compound.

Alpha 2 Delta by John Markewicz

Lt. Col Darlington: "So all of our communications gear and navigation gear is inoperative. Except man-to-man communications. We have satisfactory food, ammunition, and medical supplies. Plus, all our team members are able and available for duty and all our medical needs patients have been treated successfully."

CW5 Smith: "Yes, Sir that is correct."

Lt. Col. Darlington: "Very well. Well Done Medics! Set up defensive perimeter to include the wagon train. Staff Sergeant Amitola check on our chest wound patient. Communications, get us back in contact with somebody. Chief Smith with me, let's get some answers."

Lt. Col. Darlington and CW5 Smith go to Col. Lightlys' wagon.

Lt. Col. Darlington knocks on the side of the wagon: "Col. Lightly, may we interrupt for a moment?

Col Lightly: "You may sir."

Lt. Col Darlington: "Sir, may I ask what happened before we arrived today?"

Col. Lightly: "We were attacked by the Indians this morning, sir and have been fighting and moving all morning. We moved into this position to use the trees for cover and have water available for our people and animals."

Lt. Col. Darlington whispering to CW5 Smith: "And we showed up in the middle of it."

Lt. Col. Darlington: "So you are a group of reenactors?"

Col. Lightly: "And what is a reenactor, Sir?"

Lt. Col. Darlington smiling: "Never mind, not important. By the way what is todays date Colonel?

Alpha 2 Delta by John Markewicz

Col. Lightly: "Why June the sixth 1880, of course."

Lt. Col. Darlington: "Of Course and what is our location, Sir?"

Col. Lightly: "The Grande Ronde River in Oregon Territory. By the way Colonel Darlington, I wish to thank you for saving my daughter Cynthia's life."

Lt. Col. Darlington: "The young lady with the chest wound?"

Col. Lightly: "Yes, Sir. She would have died if not for your people. She is heartbroken however in view of the fact that my grandchildren Tyler 8 and Hailey 7 were abducted during the raid this morning."

Lt. Col. Darlington: "My sincere condolences, Sir. Would you please excuse us again Colonel?"

Col. Lightly: "Surely, Sir."

Lt. Col. Darlington and CW5 Smith are walking toward the river.

Lt. Col Darlington: "Chief call the team in, Mission Critical Briefing"

Team gathers near the river once again, far away from the wagons.

Lt. Col. Darlington addressing the team: "According to our hosts, today's date is June 6th, 1880, this body of water is the Grande Ronde River in Oregon Territory. The wagon train is enroute to Portland Oregon. They are in contact with hostile forces. They are undertaking defensive operations. In view of the one in a million chance that this is real we can't afford to kill anyone! We have no idea what impact it might have in the future. Further if we stay here and interfere any more it may change the future in any number of ways. We may have made a mistake saving Col. Lightly's daughter, full disclosure; her children one male and one female have been kidnapped by hostile forces. Opinions/observations? Speak freely."

Master Sergeant Taylor: "That's gotta' be a load of bull, Sir!"

Alpha 2 Delta by John Markewicz

Sergeant 1st Class Jakes: "They're jerkin' our chain, Sir!"

First Sergeant Watters: "This just isn't possible!"

Master Sergeant Lucas: "This is some kinda' test, Sir. Somebody's watchin' us! Recording our actions and decisions."

CW5 Smith: "Well, let's review the facts. Comms and Nav are out completely our Commo team confirms there are no satellites to connect to. A member of the play actor force is wounded severely and the rest of the crowd was just gonna' watch her die. That attack this morning was no joke either, the arrow in my pack is proof enough of that."

Master Sergeant Allen: "I didn't see anybody callin' 911."

Sergeant First Class Green; "I haven't seen or heard an aircraft of any kind all afternoon. No contrails in the sky so far today either."

Sgt. Amitola: "Well whoever they are we can't just leave them Sir. They have wounded men, women, children and animals. Plus, American Veterans both Union and Confederate on the train and if they move the Colonels daughter before she has a chance to heal a little more and gain some hydration plus receive IV antibiotics, she's gonna' die. We need twenty-four hours to stabilize her before she can be moved with any degree of safety."

Lt. Col. Darlington: "This is an unprecedented situation all opinions are important. I am going to poll the sections for advice and/or opinions."

Weapons? Sergeants Lucas and Green: "Stay."

Communications? Sergeants Black and Gronski: "Stay."

Medics? Sergeants Allen and Amitola; "Stay."

Engineers? Sergeants Taylor and Jakes; 'Stay."

Alpha 2 Delta by John Markewicz

Operations? Sergeant Major Roberts: "Stay."

Intel? First Sergeant Warren: "Stay."

Chief Smith? "We need to stay."

Lt. Col. Darlington: "It's decided then we stay with the wagon train. It is now 1800 hours. Set up defensive perimeter to include the wagon train on dismissal. Staff Sergeant Amitola stay with the Colonels daughter we'll get you the time you need. Weps make sure everyone has blanks and divide up the live 5.56 ammunition evenly between all team members except me. I have some loose 9MM pistol ammunition in my pack. REMEMBER NON-LETHAL FORCE ONLY UNLESS YOU OR A TEAM MEMBER ARE ABOUT TO BE KILLED!

The hostile force does not expect to be attacked. 0300 hours we take the war to them! Let's keep them occupied and off balance; buy the medical team some time. Dismissed!'"

Alpha 2 Delta by John Markewicz

CHAPTER 4

A2D GOES TO WAR

The team recons the area around the wagon train and sets up trip wires with trip flares and trip wires with hand grenade simulators attached. They set up ankle high trip wires across open avenues of attack and they tie handfuls of field grass together with square knots to create even more trip obstacles. They are extremely careful to camouflage each obstacle as it is installed.

They carefully inspect the area and set up Guard Posts.

The team sets 1st watch from 2000 hours to 2300 hours and those not on duty take a break. 2nd watch will be 2300 hours to 0200 hours.

 Shadow Team: Sergeants Amitola, Green, Black, Jakes, Watters, and Lt. Col. Darlington as commander are on break and they begin to get out some MRE's.

(The Meal, Ready-to-Eat – commonly known as the MRE – is a self-contained, individual field ration in lightweight packaging bought by the United States Department of Defense for its service members for use in combat or other field conditions where organized food facilities are not available. While MREs should be kept cool, they do not need to be refrigerated.)

Suddenly the children from the wagon train appear all around the team members that are on break.

They look on with interest as some team members use MRE heaters to warm their food.

(The ration heater contains finely powdered magnesium metal, alloyed with a small amount of iron, and table salt. To activate the reaction, a small amount of water is added, and the boiling point of water is quickly reached as the exothermic reaction proceeds.)

The Team members let the children share their food and hand out candy to the children when chow break is over.

Alpha 2 Delta by John Markewicz

Some of the team members begin to pull out snacks that they had purchased for themselves before the mission began.

Each soldier is going through their pack:

Sergeant Jakes has some butterscotch and some peppermint hard candy.

Sergeant Green has some potato chips and beef sticks.

Sergeant Black has some chocolate bars.

Sergeant Amitola has some cheese crackers and some peanut butter crackers.

First Sergeant Watters pulls out a box of extra-large Dog Bones. He begins to gnaw on one and the rest of the team just shakes their heads.

Ghost Team: Sergeants Lucas, Taylor, Gronski, Allen and Sergeant Major Roberts, plus Chief Smith as commander are on guard duty.

At 2300 Hours the guard detail changes, Shadow Team is on guard duty.

At 0200 Hours 1st Sergeant Watters wakes each Ghost Team member with: "Rise and shine it's O Dark Hundred!"

At 0230 Hours the team assembles.

Ghost team: Sergeants Lucas, Taylor, Gronski, Allen and Sergeant Major Roberts, plus Chief Smith as commander are to remain with the wagon train as rear guard.

Staff Sergeant Amitola stays with Cynthia to monitor her vitals and tend to her needs plus keep her resting quietly.

The rest of the team moves out to engage the hostiles. They proceed in the general direction that the hostiles chose to retreat.

Alpha 2 Delta by John Markewicz

Swiftly and silently, they move thru the terrain.

Approximately one hour later the team smells wood smoke and a little further on they detect the dim glow of camp fires in the distance.

Lt. Col Darlington: "Communications get a drone in the air and get us a visual." (The drone is like a child's remote-control airplane with a closed-circuit TV camera attached to it.)

Sergeants Black and Gronski set up and launch a drone and in a few minutes, it is hovering over the hostile camp and sending back pictures.

The images verify that the hostiles have Colonel Lightlys' grandchildren.

Lt. Col. Darlington: "Engineers can you rig us a half stick of dynamite that the drone can drop?" Communications can you rig the drone to drop the half stick on command?

Engineers and Communications: "Will Do, Sir!"

Everyone moves thru the darkness and invisibly slips into ambush position.

The team is lying prone in the grass surrounding the village.

Lt. Col. Darlington on intercom: "Fix Bayonets, just in case needed!"

They launch the drone again and a minute later the two quarters sticks are dropped into the central campfire of the hostile position.

The flash of the resulting explosion is blinding. The shock wave throws burning debris everywhere, teepees begin burning and as the hostiles run into the night the team is on them instantly, rifle butt strokes impact enemy bodies, fists fly, Army boots deliver devastating kicks, flash bangs explode completely blinding and stunning many of the hostiles. Some hostiles are forcibly disarmed and weapons confiscated.

The leader is yelling in English! It soon becomes apparent to the team he is from somewhere in Ireland based on his accent.

Green Berets materialize out of the darkness dealing stunning blows and throwing minor explosives to dazzle their opponents.

Moments later the leader of the hostile force is laying on the ground and his hands are zip tied behind his back. Overcoming his shock, he begins cursing and screaming for someone named Raven Wing to kill the white children.

Raven Wing is the leaders' squaw, she and her prisoners are running! Weapons Sergeants Lucas and Green give chase. When they are within 50 meters of Raven Wing she stops and grabs the female child and raises her knife high over her head. Weapons Sergeants Lucas and Green will not have time to change their blank magazines for live ammunition magazines. Suddenly with shocking impact and blinding speed the knife flies from Raven Wings hand and the crack of an M4A1 rifle strikes all their ears.

Staff Sergeant Amitola is visible now as the morning light intensifies. She is glaring at Raven Wing as the children run to Weapons Sergeants Lucas and Green. Staff Sergeant Amitola puts her M4A1rifle on the ground and draws her M7 bayonet. She walks up to Raven Wing and kicks her knife back to her. Raven Wing grabs for her knife and kicks sand toward Staff Sergeant Amitola's eyes and launches her body into Amitola all at the same moment. Staff Sergeant Amitola catches the full brunt of Raven Wings body block as she hits the ground rolling, now Staff Sergeant Amitola comes up to a standing position ready to fight. Raven Wing runs straight for Staff Sergeant Amitola. Amitola grabs Raven Wings knife hand and smashes Raven Wings wrist into her knee. Raven Wings knife clatters away and Staff Sergeant Amitolas' bayonet finds its mark stabbing upward under the rib cage directly into

Alpha 2 Delta by John Markewicz

Raven Wings heart as Raven Wing begins to collapse, Staff Sergeant Amitola whispers: "Only cowards attack children, Bitch!"

The rest of the team arrives at her side with their prisoner in tow.

Sergeant Green and Sergeant Lucas are each carrying a child.

Master Sergeant Lucas: "Nice shot Corpsman!"

Staff Sergeant Amitola: "Thought I'd get ready to cover your withdrawal."

Master Sergeant Allen: "Glad you were here! Who's minding our patient?"

Staff Sergeant Amitola: "Sergeant Allen is with her."

They move back to the wagon train and zip tie their prisoner to a wagon wheel.

Lt. Col. Darlington: "Chief call the team in, critical mission briefing!"

The Team is gathered in a circle a short distance from the wagon train.

CW5 Smith: "Commander – all communications are still down, tablets/cell phones are inoperative, pluggers are inoperative, GPS systems on cell phones are inoperative. Sincgars, our primary communications radio is operational but we are still unable to contact anyone. We still have 8 full 30 round magazines of 5.56 ball ammo for the M-4A1's, plus 24 full 30 round magazines of blank 5.56 ammo for the M-4A1's, 14 Grenade Simulators, 14 Artillery Simulators, 14 Flash Bangs, 24 Trip Flares, we have 36 Star Clusters: 12 Red, 12 Green, 12 White, 4 Thermite Grenades, and 40 Smoke grenades,10 red, 10 green, 10 black, 10 white, food stores are satisfactory, potable water available, all weapons fully functional, medical supplies satisfactory, no Wounded In Action,

Alpha 2 Delta by John Markewicz

One Enemy Killed In Action, no Friendly KIA's, no Missing In Action, 1 Prisoner of War.

Lt. Col. Darlington: "It's the KIA I would like to discuss. We had no alternative?"

CW5 Smith: "No Sir. Colonel Lightlys Female Grandchild was in a life threating situation at the hands of a hostile force member. Staff Sergeant Amitola had no choice"

Lt. Col. Darlington: "We have 8 full 30 round magazines of 5.56? Unless my ears deceive me, we expended at least one live round."

CW5 Smith: "You are correct Sir. Master Sergeant Lucas found one loose 5.56 round in an ammo pouch. The expended round was used to disarm the hostile.

The hostile regained the weapon in question and presented an immediate threat.

The hostile was defeated in hand-to-hand combat by Staff Sergeant Amitola"

Lt. Col. Darlington: "Well done Staff Sergeant. You can tell me about it later."

Alpha 2 Delta by John Markewicz

CHAPTER 5

WHO ARE THESE GUYS

The renegades have been attacking wagon trains and then killing and robbing the settlers at will. They are just a band of murders, thieves, and assorted criminals operating together as a gang of cut throats under the direction of one Mister Sean Harrigan.

They kill the adult males and older women, saving the young females starting at 10 years age and ending at about 25 years of age of age for sex toys and work slaves for the men of the gang. The younger children are allowed to live and are then worked/tortured to death via starvation and beatings by the women of the gang unless there is some chance to sell them for ransom.

All the stolen money and items of value are split up among the members of the gang at the direction of Mr. Harrigan.

The wagons and the animals are assigned to different families as Mr. Harrigan directs.

Some of the wagons along with the settler's furniture are collected in a hidden spot waiting to be sold at some later date.

Mr. Harrigan always gets the lion share of everything of course.

The men get their choice of the stolen weapons with Mr. Harrigan getting first choice once again.

The women of the gang go through the chests and containers of the dead taking what clothing and food stuffs they want.

Those pilgrims that are left wounded after the battle are tortured to death via target practice for the male gang members if they can still run or if hurt to bad to run by themselves, they are cut to ribbons by small slices made all over their bodies by the females of the gang until they die very slowly. Their children if they have any are made

Alpha 2 Delta by John Markewicz

to watch and if they have a female child that child is raped in front of them while they are dying.

If there is a preacher on the wagon train, he is burned alive.

Just last week they captured a wagon train and killed everyone. Made a great haul in money and guns not to mention horses and wagons plus some nice furniture.

They were a gang of about twenty plus their families more than a match for any small wagon train to fall prey to them.

This wagon train included, until their first encounter with United States Army Special Forces Soldiers.

They are now seven less gang members and every man left has some type of injury.

Alpha 2 Delta by John Markewicz

CHAPTER 6

HARRIGAN THAT'S ME

The people from the wagon train begin to gather around the team and their prisoner.

POW: "Get on with Ya'. Ya' bloody bastards!"

Col. Lightly arrives and he carefully looks over the man the team has in their custody.

Lt. Col. Darlington to POW: "YOUR NAME SIR?"

Prisoner Spits!

Lt. Col Darlington: "Sergeant Major get my Digital Camera!"

Sergeant Major Roberts: "Your Digital Camera Sir?"

Lt. Col. Darlington scowls at Sergeant Major Roberts.

Sergeant Major Roberts: "You really think it's that serious, Sir?"

Lt. Col. Darlington: "I Do!"

Sergeant Major Roberts leaves and gets the Colonels Digital Camera from his pack. Handing it to Lt. Col Darlington he says: "Per Your Command, Sir!"

Lt. Col. Darlington puts the camera right in the POW's face and takes his picture. The powerful flash at point blank range is startling. It leaves the POW blinded momentarily. The Colonel grabs the POW by the hair and shows him his picture on the digital camera viewing screen.

Lt. Col. Darlington: "I HAVE YOUR SOUL IN HERE! WANT IT BACK? START TALKING!!"

Thoroughly Frightened POW: "Name's Harrigan.

Alpha 2 Delta by John Markewicz

Lt. Col. Darlington: "You give the orders?"

Mr. Harrigan: "I'm the Boss."

Lt. Col. Darlington: "How many men do you have total?"

Mr. Harrigan: "About Twenty. Ya' killed six of 'em Ya' Dirty Bastards!"

Lt. Col. Darlington: "How many rifles?"

Mr. Harrigan: "About 18 left. We sold the rest."

Lt. Col. Darlington: "How much ammo?"

Mr. Harrigan: "To Hell with Ya'! Ya' killed six of me men Ya' Dirty Bastards!"

Lt. Col. Darlington: Hold your tongue Mr. Harrigan before I decide to make it seven!"

Lt. Col. Darlington: "Where are you from?"

Mr. Harrigan: "IRELAND YA' BLOODY FOOL!"

Lt. Col. Darlington shows Mr. Harrigan his picture again in the digital camera view screen.

Mr. Harrigan looks aghast and his knees go weak.

Lt. Col. Darlington: "How many of your men are actual Native Americans."

Mr. Harrigan: "Three or four."

Lt. Col. Darlington: "How much ammo do you have for the rifles?"

Mr. Harrigan: "30 or 40 rounds per man."

Lt. Col Darlington: "Master Sergeant Allen be sure this man is hydrated."

Alpha 2 Delta by John Markewicz

Master Sergeant Allen: "Yes, Sir."

Mr. Harrigan spots the children he abducted with Staff Sergeant Amitola and stares; he is furious!

Staff Sergeant Amitola spots Colonel Lightly in the crowd and returns his Grandchildren to him. The reunion is a loving and heartwarming event to witness. Colonel Lightly hurries the children off to see their mother.

Staff Sergeant Amitola walks over to Mr. Harrigan and whispers: "That monstrous whore that had them is dead too!"

Mr. Harrigan is Acrimonious! He begins yanking at the restrains and snarling and spitting and screaming his fury!!

Staff Sergeant Amitola holds his head while the Sergeant Major gags him.

The moment of realization that her children are returned to her unharmed is a pure amazement to Cynthia Wayne/Lightly. Tears of joy erupt from the whole family.

Sergeant First Class Jakes guides the little ones thru the maze of hoses and lines, so they can give Mom a kiss and a hug.

Colonel Lightly gives the Medic and the Engineer a nod of his head and a heartfelt, Thank You smile.

Alpha 2 Delta by John Markewicz

Chapter 7

MOVE TO CONTACT

Morning brings a spectacular sunrise and the beginning of Mission Day #2.

It also brings a group of hostile cavalry intent on recovering their leader!

CW5 Smith on intercom: "Hostiles, East, approximately 1 mile."

Lt. Col. Darlington on intercom: "Defensive positions now, remember nonlethal force only unless death is imminent. Let's out think 'em before we out fight 'em!"

The hostile cavalry starts to advance, at a trot, at a gallop, now a full charge.

The horses strike the traps and trip wires. They begin to fall throwing riders in all directions, stunned hostile soldiers are trying to recover and regain the attack.

The team opens fire with Roman Candles. Flash bangs, smoke grenades, artillery simulators, and grenade simulators sail thru the air. The ensuing flashes, whistles, and explosions are overwhelming.

 The Orange, Red, Yellow, Blue, and White balls of fire from the Roman Candles along with the Red, Green, and White Star Clusters scare the hostiles and their horses into a blind panic and a complete rout ensues with zero deaths to the hostile forces however bruises, contusions and lacerations abound.

There also seems to be some sever sprains and even some minor fractures among the hostile force per the Senior Medical Specialist Master Sergeant Allen as he monitored their withdrawal from the field.

Alpha 2 Delta by John Markewicz

Ghost Team remains on guard. Sergeants Lucas, Taylor, Gronski, Allen and Sergeant Major Roberts, plus Chief Smith as commander are on Ghost team.

Shadow Team falls back to the wagon train. Sergeants Amitola, Green, Black, Jakes, Watters, and Lt. Col. Darlington as commander are on Shadow team.

Staff Sergeant Amitola on intercom: "Col. Darlington to Col. Lightly's wagon Please Sir."

Col. Lightly is waiting for Lt. Col Darlington and they walk to his daughter's wagon.

Staff Sergeant Amitola steps down from the wagon.

Speaking in a whisper to Lt. Col Darlington: 'Sir, it would be prudent to administer a tetanus shot. However, in view of our discussion about future events is it wise to administer?"

Lt. Col. Darlington: "How critical is injection Sergeant?"

Staff Sergeant Amitola: "Should we fail to administer we could lose her anyway in spite of all we have already done."

Lt. Col. Darlington whispering: "Dam!"

Col. Lightly, stepping closer: "A problem, Sir?"

Lt. Col. Darlington: "Yes, Sir. We have a special way we use to help guard against certain illnesses it's called immunization. Your daughter needs to have this injection administered for a particular illness peculiar to this type of injury however, I fear our actions may have long term results, unforeseen results, for the future."

Col. Lightly: "I beg of you Sir. Let me keep my daughter. Allow my Grandchildren to have their Mother!"

Alpha 2 Delta by John Markewicz

Lt. Col. Darlington looking up at the sky and shaking his head: "Well, what the hell we've gone this far. Staff Sergeant administer the vaccine."

Staff Sergeant Amitola gets back into the wagon and prepares her syringes and a primary series of tetanus-diphtheria (Td) toxoid is initiated for Cynthia.

Lt. Col. Darlington is walking away.

Staff Sergeant Amitola looks out of the wagon, she sees that Lieutenant Colonel Darlington is leaving the area.

She quickly prepares three more injections and gives them to the children and Colonel Lightly.

Colonel Lightly is surprised but he comforts and quiets the children as they sniffle from the pain and the burn of the injections.

1800 Hrs. arrives and the team has given the medics the 24 hours they needed.

Lt. Col. Darlington: "Chief call the team in, critical mission briefing!"

The Team is gathered in a circle far from the wagon train.

CW5 Smith: "Commander – all communications are down, tablets/cell phones are inoperative, pluggers are inoperative, GPS systems on cell phones are inoperative. Sincgars, our primary communications radio is operational but we are still unable to contact anyone. We have 8 full 30 round magazines of 5.56 ball ammo for the M-4A1's, plus 12 full 30 round magazines of blank 5.56 ammo for the M-4A1's, 12 Grenade Simulators, 12 Artillery Simulators, 12 Flash Bangs, 20 Trip Flares, we have 30 Star Clusters: 10 Red, 10 Green, 10 White, 4 Thermite Grenades, and 40 Smoke grenades,10 red, 10 green, 10 black, 10 white, food can stretch six days, potable water available, all weapons fully

Alpha 2 Delta by John Markewicz

functional, medical supplies satisfactory, no Wounded In Action, no Killed In Action, no Missing In Action one Prisoner of War.

A new night security perimeter is arranged and emplaced.

Trip wires with flares and trip wires with hand grenade simulators are placed in likely avenues of attack or infiltration. Trip wires are strung across likely avenues of attack to act as tripping obstructions.

1st watch and 2nd watch guard duty for Ghost and Shadow Teams is scheduled.

CHAPTER 8

NOW WHAT

The morning brings another brilliant blue sky and the beginning of Mission Day # 3.

The team separates into two teams Ghost Team and Shadow team and takes up positions 100 yards away from the wagon train.

Sergeants Lucas, Taylor, Gronski, Allen and Sergeant Major Roberts, plus Chief Smith as commander are on Ghost team.

 Sergeants Amitola, Green, Black, Jakes, Watters, and Lt. Col. Darlington as commander are on Shadow team.

Blank adapters are installed, and blank filled magazines are inserted into magazine wells. M4A1 rifle bolts bang closed; dust covers click back into place. Bayonets are mounted.

Hand grenade simulators, smoke grenades, and flash bangs are passed around until every team member has some available.

The team moves out and provides a contact screen on both sides of the wagon train.

Col. Lightly has set a brisk pace and by noon the wagon train has covered ten miles.

At midday the wagon train stops for a break and a noon meal.

The team sets a defensive perimeter and breaks out snacks and some of the guys open MRE's.

All the civilians having eaten, some of the ladies from the wagon train arrive to offer coffee to the team.

Col. Lightly is running toward the team.

Lt. Col. Darlington stands.

Alpha 2 Delta by John Markewicz

Col. Lightly highly distraught: "Colonel two young people are missing from the train; I fear they have been abducted!"

Lt. Col. Darlington: "Ladies if you'll excuse us please."

Lt. Col. Darlington: "Comms get a drone in the air we have two young people missing from the wagon train."

Sergeants Black and Gronski launch a drone quickly and begin searching. As it gains altitude a wider and wider area becomes visible.

Lt. Col. Darlington watching the video feed: "Colonel there are no obvious tracks or signs of a struggle in the immediate area. No signs of a group of people moving away from the train."

Sergeant Gronski: "Colonel Darlington take a look at this sir."

Lt. Col. Darlington: "I don't see anything Sarge"

Sergeant Gronski: "Watch the large tree next to the creek sir."

Soon a partially undressed young lady appears from under the canopy of the tree branches.

Lt. Col. Darlington smiling: "Colonel Lightly if you look under a large tree along the riverbank to the west of our position approximately 1000 yards, I believe you will find two young people, uh swimming."

Col. Lightly and Matt Nilsson's Mom and Dad along with Sally Ann Andersson's parents follow the river where they discover Sally Ann on the far side of the river picking flowers.

 Col. Lightly and Matt Nilsson's Mom and Dad continue along the riverbank where they meet Matthew and Staff Sergeant Amitola swimming in their under garments.

Alpha 2 Delta by John Markewicz

Immediately Matthews parents explode in anger and demand their son gather his clothes, get dressed this instant and follow them immediately.

The Nilsson's return to their wagon with their son in tow.

Col. Lightly approaches Lt. Col Darlington with a now dressed but damp Staff Sergeant Amitola trailing.

Lt. Col. Darlington looking confused.

Col. Lightly: "Sir, I have never known a female to be in the armed forces. Now with new found experience at my disposal I demand that you hold your soldiers to a higher moral standard, Sir!"

Lt. Col Darlington looking surprised: "I was unaware any in my command had acted in any way dishonorable. I assure Sir; it will never happen again!"

Col. Lightly turns and stalks away!

Lt. Col. Darlington: "Staff Sergeant Amitola anything you would like to discuss?"

Staff Sergeant Amitola: "We were just swimming sir; and (more quietly) flirting to some degree."

Lt. Col. Darlington: "Well in this society being conservative is raised to an art; turning to the rest of the guys he says let's all be extra careful with our actions and language around these folks, people. Perhaps we should try not to generate any more problems that we already have!"

CW5 Smith: "Along those lines sir, some of the old soldiers on the wagon train have recognized and remarked on the Colt Firearms Insignia on our rifles. That's information that could make a change in their investment choices in the future, as well as lead to some discussions whose outcome I dread to consider"

Alpha 2 Delta by John Markewicz

Lt. Col. Darlington: "OK, everybody let's keep our weapons and equipment away from everyone born in this century; that's an order!"

Lt. Col. Darlington: "I'm going to apologize to Colonel Lightly."

Lt. Col. Darlington walking toward Colonel Lightly's wagon is surprised by two children, each grabbing a hand and steering him toward a wagon to the rear of Col. Lightly's wagon.

Tyler and Hailey Wayne direct Lt. Col. Darlington to their Mom. Cynthia Wayne/Lightly is resting as comfortably as possible in the current situation. She is overflowing with enthusiastic joy at being restored to her children and she credits Lt. Col. Darlington and his medical team with her miraculous recovery. She just cannot wait to express her gratitude.

Lt. Col. Darlington looking into the Wayne/Lightly wagon: "Good afternoon Ma'am, is there something I can do for you?"

Ms. Wayne/Lightly: "Please step up and visit for a moment Colonel."

Staff Sergeant Amitola steps down out of the wagon.

Lt. Col. Darlington steps up into the wagon and sits on a box next to Cynthia's bed.

Cynthia is the perfect vision of a Southern Belle. Except for the drains, the IV tubing and the oxygen feed that is being provided by the leftover bottles from the HALO jump. She is a blond, blue eyed, stunning beauty.

Ms. Wayne/Lightly: "Please excuse my being so forward Colonel inviting you into my sick room, and we never having been properly introduced."

Lt. Col. Darlington; "Not at all, Ma'am. Not at all. What can I do for you?"

Alpha 2 Delta by John Markewicz

Ms. Wayne/Lightly: "I wish to thank you, Sir."

Lt. Col. Darlington: "Any thanks should be directed to my Medical Specialists Ma'am."

Ms. Wayne/Lightly: "Oh, Colonel; Please call me Cynthia."

Lt. Col. Darlington: "Well Cynthia, I'm afraid I had very little to do with your recovery."

Ms. Wayne/Lightly: "Not so Colonel. Staff Sergeant Amitola tells me your orders could have saved me and my children or sentenced us to death. You are an exceptional man in command of a remarkable group of soldiers"

Lt. Col. Darlington: "Please promise me you won't ever mention any of this to any other human being ever!"

Ms. Wayne/Lightly: "I shall maintain my silence only if I am guaranteed of a personal relationship with you, Sir."

Lt. Col. Darlington looking shocked: "Excuse me."

Ms. Wayne/Lightly: I am told I am not unattractive and it occurs to me that a man like you would have knowledge about the future which could ensure our family of a comfortable lifestyle for generations to come. I can make you very happy for an entire lifetime, Sir. I'm afraid Sergeant Amitola and I have been conversing and it seems you are currently unattached if memory serves."

Lt. Col. Darlington: "Good Heavens!"

Lt. Col. Darlington leaves immediately and spotting Sergeant Amitola: "Sergeant personal information about soldiers in this command is CLASSIFIED, AM I CLEAR?"

Staff Sergeant Amitola: "Yes, Sir!"

Alpha 2 Delta by John Markewicz

Following another move in the afternoon the wagon train and the team set up for the night.

A standard Special Forces night defensive perimeter is set and booby traps are emplaced.

A guard roster for the Ghost and Shadow Teams is dictated by the Sergeant Major.

CHAPTER 9

YOU'RE MAKING THIS UP

Sunrise brings the beginning of Mission Day # 4.

CW5 Smith speaking to Lt. Col. Darlington: "A number of the people on the wagon train are stressing based on the fact that this morning we shall reach Deadman's Pass."

Lt. Col. Darlington: "You're making this up, right?"

CW5 Smith: "No seems this band of renegade Indians, real Indians evidently, likes to use it to ambush wagon trains going thru the place. First comes Meachem Station however. Perhaps we should leave the wagon train for that section of the journey?"

Lt. Col. Darlington: "What kind of a station is Meachem's Station?"

CW5 Smith: "Stage Coach, Sir."

Lt. Col. Darlington: "This just keeps getting better and better. I hafta' write a book! Nah, no one would believe it. Hell, I'm here and I don't believe it!! All right agreed, we send the wagon train through Meacham's station alone, we move on to Deadman's Pass and deal with that threat."

CW5 Smith: "Leave Staff Sergeant Amitola with Ms. Wayne/Lightly Sir?"

Lt. Col. Darlington: "No, I may need her. Send in Master Sergeant Allen tell him to change into civilian clothes and keep anything of ours OUT OF SIGHT and have him bury all the empty 02 bottles!"

CW5 Smith: "Yes, Sir."

Lt. Col. Darlington briefs Col. Lightly on the plan of action.

All the arrangements completed the wagon train and the team both move out.

Alpha 2 Delta by John Markewicz

The team arrives near Deadman's Pass at about the same time the wagon train is in sight of Meacham's Station.

Setting up an Observation Post on a rise just before Deadman's Pass the team begins looking for the Indians.

Lt. Col. Darlington: "Everybody Camo up." Go Hollywood, make it scary!"

In a few hours of careful maneuvering, they have the Indians surrounded.

Lt. Col. Darlington: "Staff Sergeant Amitola can you tell them they are surrounded and to come to the wagon trail?"

Staff Sergeant Amitola: 'I can try Sir."

Staff Sergeant Amitola speaking Kiowa tells the renegades they are surrounded and to have their chief go to the wagon train trail peacefully.

The Indians begin mounting horses and gathering arms.

Lt. Col Darlington on intercom: "Sergeant Green, break off the top of the chiefs spear,"

Seconds later the top of the chiefs' spear explodes and the tip goes flying away then the reverberating thunder of an Accuracy International/ Remington Arms MK-13 .300 Magnum sniper rifle echoes through the hills.

The Indians think better of the idea and the Chief with his Medicine Man move to the open wagon trail.

Quickly Lt. Col. Darlington moves to the trail and digs a small hole with the heel of his boot. He places a thermite grenade in the hole buries the grenade partially and pulls the pin.

He borrows CW5 Smiths M-4A1 rifle and mounts his own bayonet.

Alpha 2 Delta by John Markewicz

When the Chief and the Medicine Man arrive Lt. Col. Darlington asks Staff Sergeant Amitola to tell them he has the power of hell fire and he will use it to kill them, their ponies, and their families if they do not leave right now.

Staff Sergeant Amitola explains.

The Chief and the Medicine man look puzzled.

Lt. Col. Darlington nudges the grenade until the primer springs clear.

The Thermate Grenade pops and then burns at 2400 degrees centigrade (4000 degrees Fahrenheit.)

(The AN-M14 TH3 incendiary hand grenade is used to destroy equipment. It can damage, immobilize, or destroy vehicles, weapons systems, shelters, or munitions. The grenade may also be used to start fires in areas containing flammable materials. The grenade can be thrown 25 meters by average soldier. A portion of the thermate mixture is converted to molten iron, which burns at 4,000 degrees Fahrenheit. It will fuze together the metallic parts of any object that it contacts. Thermate is an improved version of thermite, the incendiary agent used in hand grenades during World War II. The thermate filler of the AN-M14 grenade burns for 40 seconds and can burn through a 1/2-inch homogeneous steel plate. It produces its own oxygen and will burn under water.)

The Indian ponies step back as the heat becomes unbearable.

Lt. Col. Darlington wearing mirror finish sunglasses and camouflage paint with his shirt sleeves down and his collar up stays as close to the grenade as he can stand.

The Chief and the Medicine Man watch astonished and must shade their eyes from the intensity of the fire as the sand is turned to glass right in front of them.

The Chief and the Medicine Man return to their camp.

The whole group packs up and begins to move west.

Alpha 2 Delta by John Markewicz

CW5 Smith standing next to Lt. Col. Darlington: "Zero casualties to team or hostiles Sir. Observation post confirms they are leaving our operational area."

Lt. Col. Darlington: "Thank God it was fold instead of raise or call!"

Alpha 2 Delta by John Markewicz

CHAPTER 10

MEACHEM STATION

Master Sergeant Allen is digging a hole under a large tree just over a slight rise where the people of the wagon train cannot see him. He is burying the empty O2 tanks that the team used on the HALO jump and then used to help Ms. Cynthia Wayne/Lightly recover from her sucking chest wound.

Returning from his task burying O2 bottles Master Sergeant Allen discovers that the wagon train is about ready to move. He jumps up into Ms. Wayne/Lightlys' wagon and changes into civilian clothes that have been donated by the members of the wagon train. Luckily his patient is asleep.

Master Sergeant Allen has had his hands full keeping Cynthia quiet and comfortable during this trip to Meachem's Station.

She has been feverish and restless the entire trip.

Master Sergeant Allen administers 800 Mg non-aspirin analgesic for pain and fever.

As the wagon train approaches Meachem's Station her plaintive sounds are detected by some folks standing near the side of the road.

Stranger: "Hey, thar, somebody sick in your wagons?"

Colonel Lightly: "Only injured, Sir."

Stranger: "Well, There's a doctor up thar aways."

Colonel Lightly: "We have tended to our wounded but we Thank You, Sir."

Stranger: "Ya' all better not be bringin' us no sickness!"

Alpha 2 Delta by John Markewicz

Colonel Lightly: "Now I have told you Sir there is no sickness on this train!"

Another stranger further up the road: "Ya' say they got sickness on that train!!"

Members of the Meachem family are gathering on the road with rifles.

Colonel Lightly: We have no sickness only wounded and we need some supplies and water for our animals and for our people, Sir."

Dylan Meachem owner/operator of Meachem Station and his oldest son Riley, both holding rifles are in the middle of the road: "You folks hold it right there!"

Dylan Meachem: "I have a wife and 12 children on this farm/way station and I can't afford no sickness to come in here!"

Colonel Lightly: "Once again Sir; we have no sickness aboard this wagon train.

The Meachem's cock their rifles as a warning.

A buggy approaches from the opposite direction.

Dylan Meachem: "Well, her comes Doc Fielding now. Let's let him decide.

Doc Fielding: 'What seems to be the trouble here?"

Dylan Meachem: "Doc it seems that this here wagon train may have some sickness a comin' along with it. They claim all they got is wounded"

Doc Fielding: "That so? {Now Yelling} Wagon Master, can ya' hear me?"

Col. Lightly: "Yes, Sir I can hear ya' fine."

Alpha 2 Delta by John Markewicz

Doc Fielding: Well then Sir, would it satisfy all parties if I had a look at the injured party?"

Col. Lightly: That would be satisfactory, Sir."

Dylan Meachem: Well, I guess I can take your word, Doc."

Doc Fielding: Well then, I'll just have a look and we can all get on with our day."

Col. Lightly: My daughters' wagon is the 5th one back doctor.

Doc Fielding; Fine Sir, that's just fine. Won't be a minute."

Master Sergeant Allen is caught by surprise. Suddenly a person is opening the back of the Wayne/Lightly wagon.

Now see here boy, I'm a doctor and I'm here to decide if this here person got a illness er' a injury.

Master Sergeant Allen has done his best to hide all the tubes and hoses leading to his patient and tucked her IV bag under her blanket but the situation demands that as the doctor is climbing into the wagon, Master Sergeant Allen must remove Cindy's O2 feed. He does so quickly and drops it on the floor while cranking the flow handle on the oxygen bottle shut. Thereby killing the now pronounced hiss caused by the escaping oxygen. He is now trying to look as innocent as a lamb.

Doctor: "Say, you got any snakes in here boy?"

Master Sergeant Allen: Don't be silly Doc, of course not!"

Doctor: "How she be doin?"

Master Sergeant Allen {in his best cowboy voice}: "She has a minor bullet wound, she gonna' be just fine Doc!"

The doctor leans over her to put his hand on Cindy's forehead and begins to move her blanket.

Alpha 2 Delta by John Markewicz

Master Sergeant Allen reaches for his Beretta 92F pistol. {If Doc sees all this, he can't let him leave!}

Cynthia Screams loud enough for everyone to hear and all the people within ear shot freeze: "Would you kindly stop leaning on my breasts you old fool!"

Doctor Fielding: "My apologies Madam!"

Old Doc Fielding: Climbing down out of Cindy's wagon as gingerly as he can: "No, no she ain't got no fever! Let 'em go!"

Master Sergeant Allen lets the hammer on his Beretta 92F go back down slowly as the doctor leaves the wagon. He looks at Cindy smiling and mouths "Thank You!"

Cindy with a big smile whispers: Couldn't let my real doctor fall on hard times, now can I?"

Master Sergeant Allen hangs the IV bag from a wagon canvas bow just high enough to maintain the flow, ties it with a zip tie, and hides it under a coat.

With all the animals watered and some minor supplies added to their meager stores the wagon train begins to move once again toward Deadman's Pass.

The wagon train stops just past Meachem's Station in an open field to rest the animals a bit and have a refreshment.

Master Sergeant Allen uses an MRE heater and an MRE main meal packet to prepare lunch for Cindy.

While Master Sergeant Allen is feeding Cindy, he notices a stage coach pass on the road.

Alpha 2 Delta by John Markewicz

CHAPTER 11

STAGECOACH

The team having delt with the Indians at Deadman's Pass decide to recon forward.

Moving west they decide to take a break and they move into the trees taking good cover on the side of the road.

The team decides to wait there for the wagon train.

They are surprised to hear wagon noises in the distance.

The wagon train could not have gotten to this point so soon.

Lt. Col. Darlington pulls 8 x 25 binoculars from his pack moves to the edge of the wooded area and peers down the road to the east.

A stage coach comes into view. It is coming down the incline from Deadman's Pass.

Lt. Col. Darlington turns to go back and inform the team of his discovery.

The sound of gunfire gets everyone's attention.

Lt. Col. Darlington picks up his field glasses for another look.

The stagecoach is being held up. Outlaws seem to have appeared from nowhere. The outlaws have guns drawn and have the stagecoach surrounded.

The rest of the team moves forward ready for battle.

Lt. Col. Darlington holds up his fist to tell the team to stop.

Communications launches a drone and the team comes closer together to watch the picture.

Alpha 2 Delta by John Markewicz

The outlaws have everyone from the stagecoach lined up and are relieving them of their valuables.

CW5 Smith: "We could intervene, Sir."

Lt. Col. Darlington: "No, we can't make contact with anymore people from this time period."

Two outlaws on horseback have everyone covered and two on the ground are collecting valuables from the stagecoach driver his shotgun rider and the passengers.

The drone video presentation shows that two outlaws collecting valuables are intent on a new prize. They are taking a very pretty, very young lady into a dense sapling and brush area. She starts to scream and cry as they drag her away ripping her clothes off as they go. The two on horseback warn everyone to stay put unless they want to die!

Lt. Col. Darlington: "DAM! Ski & Amitola save the girl! Sergeant Black, the guy on the black horse gets the drone in the face in 2 minutes. Sergeants Lucas and Green do something about that one on the paint pony!" EVERBODY REMEMBER, NO KILLS!! NO TRACE!!

 The team moves out at the double time.

Sergeants Green and Lucas arrive in the brush behind the outlaw on the paint pony silently. Sgt Lucas removes his blank adapter from the barrel of his weapon and forces a blank cartridge crimp end first into the barrel of his M4A1 rifle, takes careful aim and fires the blank cartridge that is in his weapon and the gas launches the other blank that has been jammed into the end of the barrel of his weapon as a brass rocket that impacts the side of the outlaws' head and knocks him unconscious.

Alpha 2 Delta by John Markewicz

Falling from his paint pony his gun goes skittering off into the weeds.

During that same moment the outlaw on the black horse suffers his first ever collision with a drone traveling at high speed as the frightened horse rears he is thrown and hits the ground where the wind is knocked out of him and he wears two black eyes like a racoon the result of the drone strike.

The two outlaws with the girl are completely fixated on their prize and can't bother to pay attention to what is happening back at the stage coach.

Seconds later Staff Sergeant Amitola applies a sleeper hold from behind to the outlaw that is currently getting on top of a totally nude, young women. The outlaw struggles but the pressure on his carotid artery cuts off the blood to his brain and he passes out in seconds while looking for help from his friend that is suffering the same fate at the hands of Master Sergeant Gronski.

Master Sergeant Gronski vanishes into the brush and waits to intercept any outlaws that might be coming to share in the young lady's suffering.

The young lady on the ground is still screaming. Staff Sergeant Amitola tries to calm her, then remembering that they are still wearing camo paint Staff Sergeant Amitola removes her helmet to show she is female. Using her most gentle voice she reassures the young lady and tells her to get dressed and return to the stagecoach and to forget that any of this ever happened.

The young girl gathers her clothing and runs for the stagecoach.

Staff Sergeant Amitola takes the weapons from the sleeping outlaws kicks them both in the crotch for good measure then throws the weapons far into the underbrush.

Alpha 2 Delta by John Markewicz

Lt. Col. Darlington, CW5 Smith, Master Sergeant Taylor and Master Sergeant Jakes all throw smoke grenades at the same moment and the entire scene on the road is enveloped in a super thick cloud of white smoke which covers Master Sergeant Blacks recovery of the drone, while doing so he delivers two quick blows to the outlaws' face and puts him down for the count, next he obtains the revolver of outlaw black horse. He sticks the revolver in his cargo pants pocket as he returns to Lt. Col. Darlington.

First Sergeant Watters and Sergeant Major Roberts have been working area security and keeping a sharp eye for any reinforcements arriving on scene.

Lt. Col. Darlington calls the team in via intercom.

The Green Berets dissolve into the woods and regroup at the area they chose for lunch.

CW5 Smith: "I wonder what they will make of the spent smoke grenades."

Lt. Col Darlington: "All they have is four dazed outlaws and lots questions without any answers and very few clues."

CHAPTER 12

RINSE CYCLE

The wagon train arrives into the Green Berets current area of operations and as it moves by the team, the team takes up perimeter defense lines on both sides and moves with the train.

They arrive at an area that looks as though many wagon trains have camped there before and they decide to stop for the night.

Staff Sergeant Amitola decides to wash up and wash her uniform and get the camo paint off her face and hands.

She informs the Sergeant Major of her intentions and moves stealthily and silently to the river.

She quickly undresses and dives into the river. She enjoys the luxurious cool water.

Beating her uniform and underclothes and socks on a nice bolder she finds in the stream and using a little clothes soap from a tiny bottle she has brought along, she works to remove most of today's real estate.

Getting her bar of soap and a little shampoo from a hotel size sample bottle she begins to get herself clean.

First, she pulls down a few tree limbs and hangs her clothing to dry.

A nice swim underwater completes her rinse cycle.

Standing there in the river she savors the moonlight and the night and the water.

Surprisingly another person pops up from the water.

Sergeant Amitola steels herself for an attack and prepares to defend her honor.

Alpha 2 Delta by John Markewicz

The surprise visitor proves to be Matthew Nilsson, her former patient and former recreational swimming partner.

Their eyes meet and an unspoken agreement is reached instantly.

Amitola's body is perfect, her constant physical training insures that and her youth only emphasizes it!

Her breasts are high and firm, her waist is small, her abdomen is flat and her black hair glistens almost dark purple in its damp moonlit state. Her perfect female form and enviable facial attributes make her irresistible.

Matthew's form is male perfection, a life time of hard work and minimal meals has produced a six-foot-tall young man with bulging upper arms and a six-pack abdomen with a 30-inch waist. Tan and muscular and hard beyond imagination.

The two attention starved individuals melt into each other arms. Their need overruling the warnings from parents and commanding officers.

They explore each other with light kisses and caresses. Every millimeter of skin surface on man and woman aching to be touched until their passion is overwhelming.

Their lovemaking is fast and furious, their enthusiasm does not fade after their simultaneous climax or even their second soul vibrating session, they only feel satisfied following their third experiment with each other's bodies and a final smooth but intense attempt at making love very slowly and sensuously a last ecstasy brings their young bodies and minds to a feeling of peace and glowing, fulfilling, happiness.

They stagger to the shore and collapse into each other arms savoring the embrace and closeness of each other mind, soul, and body.

Alpha 2 Delta by John Markewicz

Relaxing totally, they very nearly fall completely asleep.

The soft "shhht" as squelch is broken on her intercom alerts Staff Sergeant Amitola that she is being missed by her teammates.

Sergeant Amitola jumps up and rushes to her comm link stubbing her toe and stifling a curse with her hand, she tells the Sergeant Major everything is fine and she will be back with the team momentarily.

She hurriedly gets dressed; her body movements are mesmerizing her young partner.

She scolds him into getting dressed quickly and leaving before his parents come looking for him.

Should either family, military or civilian find them in this state they would never be able to explain it away and both their punishments would be severe indeed.

Once again dressed Sergeant Amitola is combing her gorgeous hair and Matthew buttons his shirt and comes close once again.

They hold each other intensely for a few minutes and part with a sensuous need stirring kiss.

They hold hands for a moment as they walk, finally their fingertips caress as they part ways to travel in different directions along different paths perhaps never to cross again.

Each stores a memory of the other that even huge expanses of time will never dim.

Alpha 2 Delta by John Markewicz

CHAPTER 13

CYNTHIA

The rest of the team sets up a defensive perimeter and those not on duty break open some food rations.

Staff Sergeant Amitola arrives back at the Green Beret camp site.

Master Sergeant Allen and Staff Sergeant Amitola discuss Cynthia's condition.

Master Sergeant Allen is about to leave to check on Cynthia when she arrives at the Green Beret camp site.

Cynthia Wayne/Lightly: "Colonel, may I have a word?"

Lt. Col. Darlington stands as Cynthia approaches: "Of Course Ma'am."

Cynthia and Lt. Col. Darlington begin walking toward the water and the tree covered area that Staff Sargent Amitola and young Matthew Nilsson have just vacated.

Cindy reaches for Arthur's hand. Arthur somewhat reluctantly accepts. They walk hand in hand into a moonlit area near the water.

Cindy: "I meant what I said at our last meeting Colonel."

Lt. Col Darlington: "Cynthia how old are you?"

Cindy: "Why I am 25 years of age, Sir."

Lt. Col. Darlington: "Cindy, I'm 55!"

Cindy: "That's impossible!"

Lt. Col. Darlington: "I assure you it is not."

Cindy: "Well no matter for I find you an extremely attractive man."

Alpha 2 Delta by John Markewicz

Lt. Col. Darlington: "May I say Cynthia I find you to be a stunningly beautiful young lady."

Cindy: "I fear I must sit and rest a moment now, Sir."

Lt. Col. Darlington: "Please let me help you."

As Arthur is helping Cindy to sit down her blouse becomes snagged on his Load Bearing Equipment. Holding her under the arms gently Arthur carefully lowers her into a sitting position on the soft sand, but as he stands up the buttons on her blouse pop off because the tail of her shirt is stuck in his equipment belt. Her stitches still being sensitive she is not wearing any undergarments on top and her ample breasts swing into clear view of the Colonel. Cindy makes a minor effort to cover her chest.

Lt. Col. Darlington: "Good Heavens Mrs. Wayne, I AM SO SORRY!!"

Lt. Colonel Darlington is staring but, removing his equipment vest and his uniform blouse as quickly as he can so he can give the shirt to Cindy.

Cindy: "Your tongue says you are sorry but your eyes show a level of appreciation, Colonel."

Lt. Col. Darlington: "You certainly possess an abundance of charms Mrs. Wayne."

Cindy: "Colonel my husband Captain Wayne died during the war. Please call me Cindy."

Arthur gets his uniform blouse off and kneels down in front of Cindy to help her get dressed. Cindy hesitantly lifts her left arm somewhat as her left side area is still sore to allow Arthur to put her arm into the sleeve. She watches his reaction to her bare breast carefully and now as he leans into her closely to move his shirt around her body to allow him to put her right arm into the sleeve, she makes sure to lift her right arm even a little higher to fully expose her right breast completely and once again watches for his reaction. Arthur cannot help but stare because she is simply, startlingly beautiful sitting in the moonlight, her perfect long blonde hair framing her gorgeous face and falling slightly over her perfect bare breasts. He snaps back to the mission at hand and leans his right hand on his knee as he uses his left to pull the shirt toward the middle in front as he picks up his right hand to do the same to the right side; Cindy takes his right hand in her left hand and places it on her bare right breast. She places her right hand at the back of his neck and pulls him in for to an urgent, sensuous kiss while he takes control of fondling her breast for himself.

They revel in each other savoring a kiss that lasts for minutes instead of seconds. He begins to push her back onto the sand and Cindy stops him as she says:" I don't think I'm well enough for all that just yet." Arthur seems crushed and Cindy senses his need. She says: "Just stand there for a minute soldier boy, let's see just how tough you really are." She takes him in her hand and gently strokes him back and forth while brushing him against her ample breasts. Arthur cannot stand that for long after weeks of not being with a lady and explodes all over her chest. Cindy: "My my, it has been a while hasn't it soldier boy!" He immediately pulls out some baby wipes from his uniform cargo pants pocket and gently cleans Cindy's chest and buries the evidence in the sand. He finishes dressing her and very carefully stands her up. His 6-foot 4-inch 220 Lb. frame towers over her 5-foot 5-inch 100 Lb. frame and his uniform blouse covers her down to her knees.

Cindy pulls him down for another kiss and informs him he should sleep soundly this evening. Arthur laughs quietly and agrees her prescription for his well being will definitely be effective. Cindy says: "Perhaps I have convinced you that my companionship does hold certain advantages?"

Arthur: "Definitely!"

Cindy: "May I count on future liaisons then Colonel?"

Lt. Col. Darlington: "You may indeed Mrs. Uh, Cindy."

Reaching the Green Beret camp, the rest of the team is a bit taken aback that Mrs. Wayne is wearing the Colonels uniform blouse and he is in his T-shirt.

Lt. Col. Darlington looking at the team: "She got a chill!"

Misc. Team members in the darkness: Of Course, Sir., Yes, Sir. Understood, Sir.

Lt. Col. Darlington looking into the camp: "Foxtrot Uniform Charlie Kilo, Yankee Oscar Uniform!" (The phonetic alphabet is used to spell words. Only the first letter of the proword is counted and that letter is put together with the others then used to spell another word.)

Lt. Col. Darlington: "May I see you to your wagon Mrs. Wayne."

Cindy: "But of course, Sir. How gallant of you."

Once inside her wagon Cindy kneels down for one last kiss.

As Arthur and Cindy kiss passionately the supposedly sleeping children start to giggle.

Lt. Col. Darlington: "Good Night Ma'am."

Cindy: "And a Good Night to you Sir."

Alpha 2 Delta by John Markewicz

CHAPTER 14

BIG GAME

The next morning Mission Day #5 Colonel Lightly pays a visit to the Green Beret camp site.

Colonel Lightly meeting Lt. Col Darlington and shaking hands: "Could your soldiers help with obtaining some fresh game for the people of the wagon train, Colonel.

Lt. Col. Darlington: "Yes, Sir. SFC Green."

Sergeant First Class Green: "Yes, Sir."

Lt. Col. Darlington: "The wagon train is short on fresh game Sergeant think weps can help them with that problem"

Sergeant First Class Green: "Yes, Sir."

Colonel Lightly: "Those are most unusual weapons your people carry, Sir."

Lt. Col. Darlington: "Yes Sir. May I count on your complete discretion, Sir."

Colonel Lightly: "Of Course, Sir."

Lt. Col. Darlington: Sergeant First Class Green would you be so kind as to acquaint the Colonel with the M-4A1?"

Sergeant First Class Green: 'Yes, Sir. Colonel the M4A1 5.56mm Carbine is a lightweight, gas operated, air cooled, magazine fed, selective fire rate, shoulder fired weapon with a collapsible stock. When a fully loaded twenty round magazine is inserted into the weapon and the weapon is set to full automatic fire, the M-4A1 will fire twenty rounds in two seconds, every bullet will leave the end of the barrel before the first empty shell hits the ground. The effective range of an M-4A1 Carbine is 550 yards.

Alpha 2 Delta by John Markewicz

The Enhanced Night Vision Goggle III, officially known as Rapid Target Acquisition technology allows the ENVG-III and FWS-I to work in tandem.

Green Berets manning an observation post or listening post, have thermal devices not only on their heads, but also on their weapons. A Green Beret can acquire multiple different targets at the same time and pass that information back and forth to the team. Enhanced Night Vision Goggle-III has a thermal setting that makes it effective during the day. It also offers the ability to outline silhouettes, so a Green Beret on patrol can pick out a target partially hidden by an obstacle of some kind.

We can refill your food stocks Colonel, guaranteed."

Colonel Lightly: If you would do so Sergeant, we would be ever so grateful!"

Knowing that larger game animals feed just before sunset and just after sunrise the team sets their sights on sunset.

Guarding against giving away their position the team mounts silencers to their M-4A1's.

The team travels with the wagon train all day providing contact screening on the left and the right of the route of travel.

As evening approaches the wagon train stops near a spring.

The team waits for full darkness and uses their Night Vision Goggles to spot game.

Approximately 500 yards away a small group of black tail deer emerge from the tree line to feed in an open field.

Weps and Engineers have made a bet. The guy that misses owes everybody else shooting that gets a deer Fifty Bucks!!

Alpha 2 Delta by John Markewicz

They are all going to say: "GO" on intercom when they have their targets the left most two animals belong to weps the right most two animals belong to engineers.

Sergeant Lucas-Go, Sergeant Green-Go, Sergeant Taylor-Go, Sergeant Jakes-Go.

Four M4A1 rifles emit a snap sound very quietly and First Sergeant Watters watching thru Night Vision Goggles declares all the animals fell at the same moment.

It's a tie! Each animal was hit squarely in the head and went down instantly!

Two hours later Colonel Lightly is dividing up the fresh meat of four blacktail deer among the settlers.

Everyone in the wagon train is pleased and amazed at the sudden allotment of fresh meat added to their diet.

Lt. Col. Darlington has been scouring the brush for some small game.

He can't believe his luck when he spots two turkeys.

A quick snapping sound issued by his M4A1 and a special treat for his special friend has been arranged.

Lt. Col Darlington arrives later that evening at Cindy's wagon. He has been a little busy gutting and plucking and beheading his prize.

He brings her a turkey completely ready for roasting.

Cindy and her Dad prepare the bird and everyone in the Wayne/Lightly household goes to sleep with a full tummy. (Including a visitor to their table, Arthur.)

Alpha 2 Delta by John Markewicz

The team sets guard watch. 1st watch 2100 hours to 24000 hrs. 2nd watch 2400 hours to 0300 hours. 0300 hours everybody turn to just in case.

Trip wires are emplaced.

The Engineers bring out packs of sparklers and light them in the campfire.

The people of the wagon train are amazed. The children stare astounded!

They have never seen anything like it.

The Engineer Sergeants explain the basic safety precautions to the adults.

Extremely hot, do not touch the silver area, throw in camp fire when done.

Then with parental permission the Engineers hand them out to the children and the amazed children run around merrily, laughing and giggling with their new found toys.

The joy in the children's faces is a boost to the morale of all the team members.

A moment of reprieve from the hardships these youngsters face every single day.

CHAPTER 15

THE ESCAPE

Mr. Harrigan has not been idle.

Mr. Harrigan waits for wagon the train to stop for the night so he can make good his escape.

Last evening some of the men came to help him out of the wagon to urinate and allow him a drink of water.

This is the same procedure they use at every stop during the day.

Later that same evening a different group came to feed him and allow him to relieve his bowels, same as every day and night since he was captured.

They have bedded down for the night and he is alone.

Secured in the back of a supply wagon he has been working on his plastic handcuffs and they have just broken.

He climbs down from the supply wagon silently.

He carefully and slowly moves to the tree line.

He freezes as he realizes someone is just ahead of him.

A young man relieving himself against a tree.

He must stop moving! He must stop breathing! He must stop being for this moment!

There must be no reason to raise an alarm. He cannot make a mistake.

Finally, agonizingly slowly the young man passes, returning to his bed.

Those cursed men and women in them peculiar duds is out there, somewhere.

Alpha 2 Delta by John Markewicz

They be watchin' for someone comin' not someone goin' he reasons.

Still, they are not to be toyed with!

He gets down and slithers on his belly like a snake.

He moves a few inches and stops to listen and look carefully.

Meeting one those strangers here will mean instant death, he is sure!

They will be waiting everywhere!! He forces down his panic. He begins to crawl again.

After what seems like hours, he reaches the edge of the water.

He slips into the water without the slightest noise.

He cannot believe his luck; a small log is floating down the stream.

He swims underwater toward his impromptu boat of freedom.

He raises his head momentarily for a breath and a look.

There just feet ahead!

Two or three more underwater stokes and he has a hand on the tree.

He holds on to the tree for dear life, face just barely out of the water, close against the log.

He rides the log downstream all night long.

As darkness begins to give way to a new day, he perceives he is far enough away from the wagon train and leaves his trusty log and swims to shore.

He gains the bank and there in the distance are a few of his men!

This is incredible!

They have been shadowing the wagon train hoping to free him.

Alpha 2 Delta by John Markewicz

He runs toward them and they can't believe their eyes.

Now that they have been reunited his men demand that they leave this accursed place and those devils in the strange clothes that travel with the wagon train they originally attacked nearly on week ago.

Harrigan is still worried, says he must kill the tall one to get his soul back!

The next morning the alarm is sounded all thru the wagon train but to no avail.

Mr. Harrigan has escaped!

Alpha 2 Delta by John Markewicz

CHAPTER 16

TROUBLED WATERS

Sergeant Major Roberts is waking the 1st guard watch who are now sleeping after their tour of duty. It is 0300 hours.

Sergeant Major Roberts as he shakes each man whispers "Wake up an piss the worlds on fire."

The people of the wagon train begin to stir around 0500 hours.

The Green Berets have been in work for two hours,

CW5 Smith: "Colonel this is Mission Day #6."

Lt. Col. Darlington: I see what you mean, what happens when our extraction bird shows up in our world looking for us?"

CW5 Smith: "Think we're anywhere near the original extraction point?"

Lt. Col. Darlington: "Dam if I know. Think we'll be able to see the bird if we are?"

CW5 Smith: "Hell if I know."

Cindy and some of the ladies from the wagon train arrive at the Green Beret camp site.

Each lady is bearing a gift, hot coffee, biscuits, butter, bacon, even some fruit preserves.

Lt. Col. Darlington calls the team in to partake in the repast.

CW5 Smith: "Tomorrow, according to Colonel Lightly they will reach Fort Dalles."

Lt. Col. Darlington: "Real Army Fort, huh?"

CW5 Smith: "Yea, horses, soldiers, Commanding Officer and everything. What will we do then?"

Alpha 2 Delta by John Markewicz

Lt. Col. Darlington: 'We'll decide when we get there I guess."

Staff Sergeant Amitola walks down to the wagon train to check on Cindy's children.

She finds Colonel Lightly reading to the children as they start out their day in his wagon.

Colonel Lightly and the children are doing well after a slight reaction to the primary series of tetanus-diphtheria (Td) toxoid vaccine that Staff Sergeant Amitola Administered.

The Wayne/Lightly family had some sniffles, slight fever overnight, a little achy the next day as their reaction to the vaccine.

Ghost team goes on guard duty and Shadow team begins cleaning weapons.

Every soldier knows that if you take care of your rifle it will take care of you.

Some guys are still sipping warm coffee from their canteen cups while they service their weapons.

The Engineers make a quick inventory of ammo and explosives.

Hand Grenade Simulators, Artillery Simulators, and Smoke Grenades are redistributed so that all team members have access to available supplies.

Medical/Surgical kits and medical supplies are inventoried and the Medics balance their available supplies between them.

There are two oxygen bottles that still have a percentage of their full charge available and these are split between Master Sergeant Allen and Staff Sergeant Amitola.

Commo equipment is cleaned, tested, and inventoried.

Binoculars and Night Vision Equipment are cleaned and checked.

Alpha 2 Delta by John Markewicz

Lt. Col. Darlington cleans his sidearm and goes thru his pack. There he discovers a full magazine of live 9 MM ball ammo plus six loose rounds for his Barretta 92F pistol.

Three hours later guard detail is switched and the other half of the team performs maintenance duties on their weapons and equipment.

The wagon train begins to move and the team takes up contact screening positions on both sides of the wagon train about one hundred yards out on either side.

Just a few hours into the day the wagon train comes to a creek. It must have rained heavily in the mountains because the creek is running deep, fast, and wild.

The normal fording point is impassible.

Lt. Col. Darlington on intercom: "Engineers forward."

Master Sergeant Taylor and Master Sergeant Jakes appear at Lt. Col. Darlington's' side in just a few minutes.

Lt. Col. Darlington: "Can you get us across this gentleman?"

Master Sergeant Taylor: "Sir, with the help of the men on the wagon train we can cross in a few hours."

Lt. Col. Darlington: "Colonel Lightly will your people assist?"

Colonel Lightly: "Most assuredly, Sir."

Lt. Col. Darlington: "Staff Sergeant Amitola stay with the bridging party in case of an accident the rest team will provide security for the bridging operation."

The Engineers and the people from the wagon train dive into the task.

First, they find three large trees that are at least forty feet high.

Alpha 2 Delta by John Markewicz

Cutting these trees down, they clean off all tree limbs.

Next, they drag them to a narrow spot in the course of the creek where the banks are close together.

Using one tree as fulcrum they angle another tree out until it reaches past the other bank, then let it down.

When two trees are across and placed side by side. Master Sergeant Taylor and half the men from the wagon train cross the creek.

The team on the East bank slide the third tree across on the other two trees that are already in place. This allows the team on the West bank to assist in the tree placement.

Each team now locates a tree that is at least thirty feet high, they cut it down, trim off all the branches and place it under the end of the three logs that are over the creek.

They space the three trees equally across the thirty-foot bridge abutment cross tree and notch the logs so the fit together firmly using pieces from the stumps of the cut trees to act as shims where needed.

Each bridge team locates trees that are approximately twenty-five feet tall.

They cut them down and remove all the limbs, then split the tree in half.

Each tree half is laid on the three logs that go over the water and notched to fit into the space as needed to act as the bridge deck.

The teams do not trim the ends as most overhang on the left or right or both.

The men use parachute cords cut from the parachutes the members of the wagon train collected and took with them for their personal use at some later time and use it to lash the timbers of the bridge together as they go.

They fill in the bridge abutments to the roadway with dirt to make it a smooth approach and departure from their newly constructed bridge.

The project takes the men over eight hours of hard work to complete.

The wagon train crosses the bridge and sets up camp on the other side as everyone needs a rest.

The ladies of the wagon train prepare the evening meal and the Engineers and Staff Sergeant Amitola are invited join in.

Master Sergeant Taylor and Master Sergeant Jakes are removed from the duty roster for tonight per Sergeant Major Roberts.

The team sets guard watch. 1st watch 2100 hours to 24000 hrs. 2nd watch 2400 hours to 0300 hours. 0300 hours everybody turn to just in case.

Trip wires and tripping obstacles are emplaced.

Lt. Col Darlington asks Colonel Lightly to collect the parachutes and burn them as soon as possible.

The youngest boys of the wagon train have been sent to fish further up river, while the men and older boys help the engineers build a bridge.

The Weapons Sergeants go along for security.

After a few hours with no luck catching fish the Weapons Sergeants decide enough is enough.

They call the children over to them.

Alpha 2 Delta by John Markewicz

Sergeants Lucas and Green leave them in a group with strict orders not to move until they are told to move.

The Sergeants walk up stream about 100 yards and throw in two hand grenade simulators as far up stream as they can throw.

The simulators explode under water and fish and eels begin floating to the top.

The Sergeants yell down to the boys to wade into the water and take the ones they want.

When they arrive at the boy's location the young men are astounded and their baskets are full of fish.

The Sergeants just look amused and say: "That's how Special Forces Soldiers Fish!"

Alpha 2 Delta by John Markewicz

CHAPTER 17

OPS DAY 7

Sergeant Major Roberts is waking the 1st guard watch who are still sleeping after their tour of duty. It is 0300 hours.

Sergeant Major Roberts as he shakes each man whispers "Turn To - time to scratch your watch and wind your ass."

CW5 Smith: "Sergeant Major this is Mission Day #7."

Sergeant Major Roberts: "I'll remind the Colonel, Chief."

Lt. Col. Darlington standing, yawning: "Another beautiful summer morning, Sergeant Major."

Sergeant Major Roberts: "Chief Smith wants me to remind you, this is Ops Day 7, Sir."

Lt. Col. Darlington: "Roger That, Sergeant Major."

The team members are checking weapons and equipment.

Suddenly a trip flare pops, then another goes off.

The team takes up defensive positions.

Night Vision Goggles which are mounted on the Green Berets helmets are snapped down into place and reveal hostile forces moving thru the high grass

The predawn orange tinted white glow of sunrise begins to break on the horizon.

Night Vision Goggles are retracted back into the helmet mounts.

Lt. Col. Darlington: "Fire White Star Clusters!"

10 White Star Clusters burst in the air and the hostile force becomes frightened and begins to fall back.

Alpha 2 Delta by John Markewicz

A full spread of Roman Candle fire directed straight toward them encourages their retreat.

In full retrograde action the hostiles face plant as they strike other trip wires and fall face first into mother earth.

The screams and yells coming from the wagon train indicates a flanking maneuver by a portion of the hostile force.

Shadow team melts away from the current contact line and appears in around, under, about the settlers and their wagons and animals.

Enemy rifle fire and arrows are starting to become effective as the light increases.

Noting the location of the rifle barrel flashes Shadow team throws six black smoke grenades and as the smoke density increases, they move out at a crouching run. When they are in the clear and running low toward the enemy line, they all throw flash bangs and fall face down. The six explosions are deafening the flashes are blinding. The Green Berets are on their adversaries in moments some are disarmed and struck with their own weapons, some are struck by US Army M4-A1's, some are defeated in hand-to-hand combat. Some escape.

The four captured hostiles have their mouths duct taped and wrists zip tied behind their backs. They are returned to the wagon train and zip tied to wagon wheels.

Special Forces Intel Sergeant Watters: "Colonel Darlington we have four POW's *(Prisoners of War)*. That would leave Mr. Harrigan with total battle force of approximately 14. Confiscated weapons, ammo, and equipment were turned over to Colonel Lightly, Sir."

Lt. Col. Darlington speaking to CW5 Smith: "Chief we gotta' get 'em to Fort Dalles!"

Alpha 2 Delta by John Markewicz

The team does not realize that they are the target and that to get his soul back Mr. Harrigan is willing to kill everyone and anyone but particularly Lt. Col. Darlington.

Lt. Col. Darlington speaking to CW5 Smith: "Let's see Colonel Lighlty and get this circus on the street!"

CW5 Smith: "Roger That Sir!"

The team splits into Shadow and Ghost teams and takes up defensive screening positions about 100 yards away from the wagon train on the left and right.

The wagon train begins moving toward Fort Dalles.

The hostile force shoots at the Green Berets from hidden positions all along the route of march but they never return fire.

After Sergeant Major Roberts is grazed Lt. Col. Darlington orders the team to lock and load live ammunition into their M4A1's. However, rules of engagement are to shoot to disarm or wound only!

Communications team launches their drone to search for hostile forces locations.

Colonel Lightly sets a brisk pace as the wagon train makes a run for Fort Dalles.

Shots are traded all day and lunchtime comes and goes without notice on this day.

A hostile soldier running for his horse is spotted by Sergeant First Class Green who wounds the hostile in the leg.

As a hostile soldier takes aim from a sniper perch in a tree, Master Sergeant Lucas spots the movement of the rifle barrel in the leaves of the tree and wounds that hostile in the forearm, his adversary loses his weapon and falls from the tree.

Alpha 2 Delta by John Markewicz

Intelligence Sergeant Watters informs Lt. Col. Darlington that counting suspected and confirmed wounding of hostile forces so far today Mr. Harrigan has approximately ten fully functional soldiers left. The team has suffered one minor wound to Sergeant Ski (Gronski) from communications. The medics have patched up his butt cheek and he is now riding shotgun for Colonel Lightly the team and the wagon train have one Wounded in Action, no Killed in Action and no Missing in Action.

One former Union Soldier and One former Confederate Soldier are guarding the four Prisoners of War and have them tied to the back of a wagon.

The team has been using coordinated smoke grenade deployments to shield the movement of the wagon train through open areas.

Data from the drone has provided the team with ambush location intelligence

Team members have been running ahead of the main body to engage ambush locations and have managed leave two more of Mr. Harrigan's force tied up and gagged in the forest.

According to Intelligence Sergeant Watters the current hostile force comprises seven or eight. Four of that number are suspected of having serious wounds.

It is late in the afternoon now and Fort Dalles is barely visible in the distance.

CHAPTER 18

FORT DALLES

Lt. Col. Darlington on intercom: "Team assemble at rear of wagon train."

The team assembles for quick situation review.

Lt. Col. Darlington: "The wagon train is coming to Fort Dalles and we will be directly under command authority if we enter. Thoughts? Speak freely!"

CW5 Smith: "The wagon train no longer needs us. We can cover them all the way to the fort from here."

Sergeant Major Roberts: "We should avoid contact with command authority at all costs for as long as possible!"

Intelligence Sergeant Watters: "He's right Sir. Direct contact with the United States Army in 1880 with this kind of equipment could have all kinds of unforeseen ramifications."

Lt. Col. Darlington: "We are agreed then, we wait here for the situation to develop?"

Every Green Beret in the team nods approval.

Lt. Col. Darlington: "I need to inform Colonel Lightly!"

Lt. Col. Darlington starts running for Colonel Lightlys wagon.

Suddenly Staff Sergeant Amitola is right next to him. She says: "Need to check Cindy's wagon for medical equipment she could never explain Sir."

Lt. Col. Darlington: "Roger that Sarge. Quick as you can! Collect Sergeant Gronski too"

Staff Sergeant Amitola: "Will do Sir!"

Alpha 2 Delta by John Markewicz

Lt. Col. Darlington jumps into Colonel Lightly's wagon and explains the situation to the colonel. Colonel Lightly says he understands. They shake hands and Lt. Col. Darlington steps down out of the back of the wagon. He stands fast for a minute and steps up into Cindy's wagon. Staff Sergeant Amitola is already gone and she is helping Sergeant Gronski to the ground as Colonel Lightly slows for just a moment. Arthur steps up to the front of Cindy's wagon and takes off the solid platinum ring with blue/white diamonds he has purchased as an investment in his own time and slips it on Cindy's finger. This should take care of you and the kids for quite a while. He kisses her and they part.

Cindy's eyes fill with tears.

Staff Sergeant Amitola has collected anything that could be a problem from Cindy's wagon and she next runs to find Matt Nilsson.

Matt jumps down from his wagon. He and Sergeant Amitola embrace and she presses her gold heart shaped necklace into his hand. She whispers: "Never Forget Me!"

They part and Matt runs to catch up with his parents.

Shockingly the Sincgars radio springs to life and Ghostrider is calling Alpha 2 Delta.

Seconds later the team can hear the helicopter landing in the distance and they see the shaking of tree tops as the rotor wash approaches.

They begin to move toward the sound and incredibly there is a fog bank in a low-lying area just off to their right.

The team is now running in that direction.

The whiz and crack of bullets flying around them gets their attention.

Alpha 2 Delta by John Markewicz

Throwing the last of their smoke grenades they attempt to cover their withdrawal.

The enemy cavalry moves forward.

Mr. Harrigan wants that thing that has his soul from that tall bastard!

The closer the team gets to the sound they realize that the aircraft is just across a small bridge in a clearing.

The closer they get to the bridge the faster the cavalry begins to close on them.

Communications Sergeant Black is with Lt. Col. Darlington and hands him the radio handset: "Ghostrider this is Delta 06, Crew Chief fire over the cavalry's heads! Scare them off!"

Amazingly orange footballs are flying toward the enemy cavalry, these 50 caliber tracers have five regular 50 caliber bullets between each one of them. The door gunner/crew chief aims high and trees begin to explode into pieces and tree limbs and leaves/ pine needles fly everywhere.

Mr. Harrigan believing it is just some new kind of trick. He stands on his saddle to catch an orange ball because they are just like the Roman Candles, they have been shooting at them all day, and a 50-caliber bullet knocks him off his horse killing him instantly.

The hole in his body is massive!

The frightening death of Mr. Harrigan sends the balance of his gang running for the hills.

Crossing the bridge, the Green Beret team boards the helicopters.

A wounded Master Sergeant Nick Gronski being aided by Master Sergeant Johnny Allen and Staff Sergeant Amitola.

Alpha 2 Delta by John Markewicz

Aircraft Commander on radio: "What the hell was that all about, Sir?"

Lt. Col. Darlington: "Long Story A/C. Tell ya' all about it at the Officers Club."

Alpha 2 Delta by John Markewicz

CHAPTER 19

NSA

As the helicopters lift off for Fairchild Air Force Base in Washington the team begins to relax. Everyone is looking forward to a hot shower and a cold beer.

CW5 Smith and Lt. Col. Darlington are looking at each other.

CW5 Smith: "What are we gonna' say in the After-Action Briefing?"

Lt. Col. Darlington: "No matter what we say about the last 7 days nobody will ever believe it."

CW5 Smith: "What are we gonna' say at the hospital pad about Gronski?"

Lt. Col. Darlington: "The Boy Scouts ambushed us! Perfectly good Master Sergeant Shot in The Ass!"

Commanding Officer and Executive Officer have a good laugh.

Landing at the base hospital Master Sergeant Gronski is spirited away on a gurney for examination and further treatment.

After explaining to the After-Action Briefing Officers what had happened, the team was housed in the base stockade.

Everyone believes that they blew off the Boy Scouts and went on a week long drunk and accidently shot one of their own.

When it is confirmed that the bullet that struck Master Sergeant Gronski was a 30 caliber the Base Officers begin to take the account a little more seriously.

The National Security Agency sends agents to review the case with the team.

Extensive video recordings of interviews are taken.

Alpha 2 Delta by John Markewicz

Multiple signatures are demanded by the NSA personnel.

They stay in the stockade for their last thirty days and must sign a gag order from a Federal Judge before that can be discharged.

They are allowed to leave the stockade at one-hour intervals and are warned by NSA never to contact each other again!

Staff Sergeant Amitola is retired from the U.S. Army and immediately appointed an NSA medical assistant employed at a black ops site.

Finally released from the hospital and discharged from the United States Army Master Sergeant Nick Gronski starts to write a book about the incident. He spends thirty days in a Maximum-Security Federal Prison and changes his mind about the book.

Arthur Darlington is offered the job of security consultant at the Vinnell Corporation. A company known for its CIA connections.

Dean Smith becomes a Senior Manager at Halliburton.

All the Sergeants are hired as civilians by various U.S. Government Agencies all at the GS-09 level or above.

Every member of the team is right where NSA wants them completely under control.

BIBLIOGRAPHY

DEPARTMENT OF THE ARMY United States Trial Defense Service Fort Rucker Field Office 5700 Novosel St, Room 345 Fort Rucker, AL 36362. ARTICLE 15

C-17 Globemaster III > U.S. Air Force > Fact Sheet Display (af.mil)

FM 3-05.211 (FM 31-19) MCWP 3-15.6 NAVSEA SS400-AG-MMO-010 AFMAN 11-411(I) Special Forces Military Free-Fall Operations

https://military.wikia.org/wiki/Precision_Lightweight_GPS_Receiver

https://military.wikia.org/wiki/SINCGARS

https://military.wikia.org/wiki/Smoke_grenade

Army FM 23-30 Grenades and Pyrotechnic Signals

Roman candle (firework) from Wikipedia, the free encyclopedia

Cherry bomb from Wikipedia, the free encyclopedia

M-80 (explosive) from Wikipedia, the free encyclopedia

Sparkler from Wikipedia, the free encyclopedia

Firecracker from Wikipedia, the free encyclopedia

Alpha 2 Delta by John Markewicz